P9-AZX-671

"Come on!" Luke grabbed Melanie's arm and pulled her toward the trees on the side of the road where they could hide out of view.

"Maybe it's someone who will help us!" she said excitedly.

"Maybe," he said. Or maybe it was the shooter. Or an accomplice of the shooter. They had no proof that the assailant was acting alone.

Headlights rounded a twist in the road, washing Luke's disabled truck in light, and then the vehicle stopped. It stayed on the road, engine idling.

After a few seconds it crept forward a little. And in the wash of the illumination from the headlights, the front of the rig became visible.

Beside him, he heard Melanie draw in a sharp breath.

"That truck looks familiar," she whispered.

It looked familiar to Luke, too. He readied his gun, flicking off the safety, just in case. Then he pointed his flashlight toward the windshield of the truck and turned it on.

Jenna Night comes from a family of Southern-born natural storytellers. Her parents were avid readers and the house was always filled with books. No wonder she grew up wanting to tell her own stories. She's lived on both coasts, but currently resides in the inland Northwest, where she's astonished by the occasional glimpse of a moose, a herd of elk or a soaring eagle.

Books by Jenna Night

Love Inspired Suspense

Last Stand Ranch
High Desert Hideaway
Killer Country Reunion
Justice at Morgan Mesa
Lost Rodeo Memories

Visit the Author Profile page at Harlequin.com for more titles.

LOST RODEO MEMORIES

JENNA NIGHT

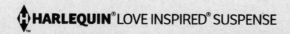

If you purchased this book without a cover you should be aware that this book is stolen property. It was reported as "unsold and destroyed" to the publisher, and neither the author nor the publisher has received any payment for this "stripped book."

Recycling programs for this product may not exist in your area.

LOVE INSPIRED BOOKS

ISBN-13: 978-1-335-67972-7

Lost Rodeo Memories

Copyright © 2019 by Virginia Niten

All rights reserved. Except for use in any review, the reproduction or utilization of this work in whole or in part in any form by any electronic, mechanical or other means, now known or hereafter invented, including xerography, photocopying and recording, or in any information storage or retrieval system, is forbidden without the written permission of the editorial office, Love Inspired Books, 195 Broadway, New York, NY 10007 U.S.A.

This is a work of fiction. Names, characters, places and incidents are either the product of the author's imagination or are used fictitiously, and any resemblance to actual persons, living or dead, business establishments, events or locales is entirely coincidental.

This edition published by arrangement with Love Inspired Books.

® and TM are trademarks of Love Inspired Books, used under license. Trademarks indicated with ® are registered in the United States Patent and Trademark Office, the Canadian Intellectual Property Office and in other countries.

www.Harlequin.com

Printed in U.S.A.

But the Lord is faithful, who shall stablish you,
and keep you from evil.
−2 Thessalonians 3:3

To my mom, Esther.

ONE

"She's alive!"

Melanie Graham wasn't sure if she just heard someone yell something, or if she'd been asleep and dreaming. Feeling groggy, she lifted her heavy eyelids and found herself gazing at a dark night sky, dotted with spiky silver stars. Her view was silhouetted with pine-tree branches high overhead that shifted back and forth in the cool, swirling breeze.

That was odd.

When she'd gone to sleep last night, it was in a bed in a hotel room. Her lodgings were across the street from the Community Attractions Arena in Leopold, Wyoming. After three hectic days the Wild Ride Rodeo had come to an end. She'd carefully packaged up all the jewelry she had left in the sales booth she'd rented in the merchandise-and-concessions area—and there wasn't much left over, as sales had been good—and then she'd gone to her hotel to relax and get a good night's sleep. She distinctly remembered setting her alarm so she could wake up early and start the four-hundred-mile drive back home to Bowen, Idaho, just as the sun came up. So what was she doing lying on the ground?

"Ma'am, are you Melanie Graham?"

She shifted her gaze to look at the young man kneeling on the ground beside her. He was holding a flashlight and wearing a jacket with the words Event Security written across the front in big silvery reflective letters.

Apparently he'd been talking since she'd first opened her eyes, but his words hadn't registered. The sound of them was like hearing someone speak on TV, in another room, when she wasn't watching the program. It felt like what he was saying had nothing to do with her.

Except, maybe it did. Whatever was happening right now wasn't a dream. It was *real*.

A jolt of terror shot through her chest, and she sat up, screaming and trying to crawl backward, away from the man, even though she wasn't sure why. The sudden movement made her head spin, throwing off her balance until she found herself pathetically crawling on her side, tearing her hands on exposed rock and pine cones and tree roots, but she didn't care. From deep inside something screamed at her that she *had* to get away.

A second man stepped through the trees, into the small clearing. He was bigger than the event security guy. He, too, carried a flashlight. When he got closer, she could see the light shining on a badge, and that he wore the uniform of a Miles County, Idaho, deputy sheriff. The county where her home was located. It was one more thing that didn't make sense.

Confusion made her head pound. And then she realized something else was making her head pound. It actually felt sore.

"Confirm, we've found Melanie Graham," the deputy said in a deep voice into his collar mic. "Get emergency medical services moving toward my location."

At the same time Melanie reached up to touch her sore, aching head. Her hair felt damp. Even before she looked at her fingertips in the glow of the two flashlights, she knew by the coppery scent that she'd touched blood.

What had happened to her?

Her body began to tremble. Her head started to spin even faster. She couldn't catch her breath.

"Melanie." She heard the deputy say her name, but she couldn't stop staring at the blood on her fingers. Couldn't stop trying to peer past the shrouded memories in her mind and figure it out. How did she get here?

"Melanie." The deputy's deep voice was louder now and it broke through her trance. She turned to him. He crouched beside her. Dark hair, dark eyes, the expression on his face focused and thoughtful, yet compassionate at the same time. "You're safe," he said.

Safe from what?

"I'm Lieutenant Luke Baxter," he said. "I'm a deputy sheriff." He reached out his hand, but didn't actually touch her. He waited for her to make the first move.

Finally she took his hand. "What happened?" she asked, struggling to sit up.

"Wait," he cautioned, while holding up his other hand in a staying gesture. "It would be better for you to wait until the medic checks you out before you start moving around too much."

"What happened to me?" she repeated.

He lifted an eyebrow. "I was hoping you could tell me."

"I don't even know where I am." Her voice caught and she could hear a sob rising up in her throat. She'd never felt so lost in her life.

The deputy squeezed her hand a little tighter. His touch, along with the feeling of calm and strength emanating from him, made her feel a little less panicked. "You've obviously sustained a substantial blow to your head," he said. "That can leave anybody addled. We'll get you to a doctor as soon as we can."

She heard tree branches snapping, boots stomping on hard-packed dirt, and people talking, and then an emergency medical crew stepped through the trees and into the clearing.

"What's the last thing you can remember?" the deputy asked.

Melanie got the impression he was in more of a hurry now. That he wanted to get all of the information he could from her before the paramedics transported her to the hospital.

She tried hard to think back, but the last thing she could remember was being in the hotel in Wyoming. A flare of panic threatened to push the sobs she'd been swallowing back up to the surface again. Tears formed in the corners of her eyes. She squeezed the deputy's hand a little harder, because right now he seemed like the only certain thing in her life. The only anchor she could hold on to.

Which was crazy, because she'd only just met the man. But she didn't want to face any more strangers right now. Didn't want to feel any more bewildered and overwhelmed than she already did.

"Oh, dear Lord," she began to pray softly, uncertain what she would say next. And immediately the thought came to her. *I will be with you always.*

She was never alone, even if she felt alone. How many times had she reminded herself of that over the last couple of years, as she'd pieced her life back together? *Lots* of times. Her lungs were tight with fear, but she managed to take a deep breath and blow it out. She loosened her grip on the deputy's hand without actually letting go of him and answered the paramedic's questions as best she could.

During pauses in her conversation with the medic, Melanie spoke to the deputy. "The last thing I remember is going to sleep in my hotel room in Wyoming."

By his long silence she could guess he was trying to decide what he should say to her.

"I realize I must be back home in Miles County," she said.

"Where do you live?"

"In Bowen." The biggest city in the county. Which didn't mean it actually was a big city. Some people probably wouldn't call it a city at all.

They were interrupted while one of the medics talked to her, shined a pen light in her eyes several times and felt around for any apparent broken bones. Her head still pounded, but at least the dizziness had subsided.

"You aren't far from town," Luke said while the medic called in to the county hospital's emergency room, with an update on Melanie and a request for further directions. "You're in the woods just south of the county fairgrounds."

"Oh, that's a weird coincidence," she said. "I'm going to have a booth there, where I'll sell my jewelry during the rodeo in a couple of weeks."

"Tonight was the last night," Luke said.

"Of the rodeo? How can that be? It's two weeks in the future."

"It ran this past week, as scheduled."

So she'd lost *two weeks* of her life? That wasn't possible. Panic started to raise its ugly head again. She could feel her heartbeat speeding up. Her face getting warmer.

"How did you know to come out here, into

the woods, looking for me?" she asked, not certain she wanted to hear the answer.

Once again he took his time in answering. Probably concerned any information he gave her might traumatize her even more.

"Please tell me," she said as calmly as she could. "I have a pretty vivid imagination. And sometimes that isn't a good thing."

He tilted his head slightly. "You had an assistant working your booth with you."

"I always do that. So I can take a break without having to lock everything up." And then a terrible thought crossed her mind. "Peter Altman. Is he all right?" She held her breath while waiting for the answer.

Melanie rented space to sell her handmade jewelry, as well as antiques and small pieces of restored furniture, in The Mercantile, downtown. Peter was a year out of high school, looking to work as many hours as he could to save money for college. The owner of The Mercantile had recommended Peter, and it had worked out great.

Luke nodded. "The rodeo was over. Many of the vendors had already cleared out. You'd packed up your inventory and were ready to leave when you gave Peter permission to grab something to eat."

"A lot of the food sellers will give away leftover cooked food rather than throw it in the trash, when they're closing up." Melanie was trying to picture what Luke was telling her. And trying to guess what he would say happened next. Maybe even *remember* what happened next. But she couldn't.

"Peter was surprised when he came back and you weren't in your truck, waiting for him. And worried. He tried to call you on your phone, but you didn't answer. Then he started literally calling out for you, all around the exhibition hall, where you'd been located, and then outside.

"He got event security out searching for you. And then one of the searchers heard gunshots from this direction. Several people called in, reporting they'd heard gunfire, and I got here as quickly as I could."

Melanie stared at him, trying to take in everything he was telling her. None of it seemed the slightest bit familiar. Moving slowly and feeling a little bit queasy, she once again reached her hand up to her head. "Have I been shot?"

Luke looked to the medic who'd been taking her initial assessment.

"Melanie, we need to roll you onto this backboard," the medic said in response. "Once we get you checked out at the hospital, we'll have all the facts."

"I can probably walk," she said.

"No, we don't want you to do that," he responded. "We don't want you walking until we know the extent of your injuries."

She turned to Luke as he slowly let go of her hand. "I need to get to work on finding out exactly what happened to you," he said. "But first I have to ask, do you have any enemies? Anyone you think could have done this?"

"No."

"Has anyone ever threatened to harm you? Kill you?"

"No."

His questions seemed ridiculous. But then the seriousness of his line of reasoning began to sink in. Was it really possible someone had wanted to *kill* her? Why?

And if so she had no idea who that person might be. Which meant they could walk right up to her and try to kill her again. And the next time she might not be able to get away.

"Is this all you have for security footage of the parking lot?" Luke asked impatiently. "It's not much help."

"That's all there is, Lieutenant." Don Chastain, the chief of event security for the fairgrounds, rubbed his hand over the sprinkling of gray stubble on his chin. They were standing in his office.

"Luke, you've responded to calls here before," Don added. "You know our biggest problem is geniuses trying to break into the exhibition halls or the main office, in the middle of the night, because they apparently think we store chests full of gold in there." He shook his head. "Normally we just deal with your garden-variety foolishness. And drunk and disorderly, of course. We've never had to worry about people getting *shot* at before."

Biting back his impatience Luke once again watched the shadowy, low-quality video of the parking lot. Just in case he'd missed something the other three times he'd watched it.

He hadn't. The single fixed camera was focused on a section of the parking lot, far from the spot where Melanie Graham was seen standing beside the cab of her pickup truck, prior to the attack. The images didn't show anything notable. Just people walking to their vehicles and leaving.

All right, that was a dead end. Time to try something different. Luke turned to the rail-thin eighteen-year-old kid standing a couple of feet away from him. Technically being eighteen made the guy a man. But dressed in an oversize green-and-white plaid flannel shirt and sharply creased blue jeans, sporting a big silver belt buckle, he really did look like a six-foot-tall boy.

"Peter, did you see anybody walking up to Ms. Graham when you left to get something to eat?"

"No, sir."

"Any odd behavior on her part? Did she seem worried or nervous?"

Peter shook his head.

Luke was hoping to get some kind of lead quickly. Right now one team of deputies was searching through the woods, trying to pick up any trail of a fleeing perpetrator. A second team, together with two forensic specialists, was combing the area where Melanie Graham had been found.

Once Melanie had been driven away in the ambulance, Luke had gone looking for Peter. So far he was the closest thing Luke had to a witness. But the kid was under-standably shaken up. Hoping he'd be able to offer some useful information once he'd calmed down, Luke had asked him to hang around for a bit.

"I guess the guy got away with all Ms. Graham's money," Peter said, shaking his head sadly.

"It wasn't a robbery," Luke said. Or if it was meant to be a robbery, it wasn't suc-cessful. Melanie's purse had been recovered from her truck, complete with her wallet, phone and about forty dollars in cash. He'd seen it for himself, and he'd tucked the purse beside her, on the backboard, after she'd been loaded into the ambulance.

"So, I guess that means you found the

lockbox?" Peter asked, raising his eyebrows hopefully.

"What lockbox?"

"A blue metal box she had on the front seat of the truck."

Luke had looked through the truck and arranged for both the truck and trailer to be securely stored at the fairgrounds until Melanie could have someone come get them. The trailer had been closed up, with padlocks threaded through the door latches, and there was no sign that anyone had tried to break into it.

"What did she keep in the lockbox?" Luke asked. "Money? Her receipts for the day's sales?"

"Yes," Peter said. "She also put some of her more expensive jewelry in there. The things she made out of gold. There's not very much of that. Most of it is silver."

If the thief tried to pawn the stolen jewelry, that would give them the start of a lead on who they were looking for.

Maybe what happened to Melanie Graham tonight was a simple strong-arm robbery, but it seemed odd. There were several other vendors who would have pulled in a lot more money, particularly the food-and-drink sellers, who typically dealt in cash.

There was that small window of opportunity when Peter went to get food and Melanie was left alone, but who would have known she'd have cash and be by herself at that exact moment?

So, what might have happened? Somebody walked by at just the right time, saw their opportunity and tried to rob her? She grabbed the box and ran, and they chased her and then shot at her? For an unknown amount of money? With witnesses around?

That was hard to believe. But anything was possible. And he really wanted to catch whoever had done this.

Luke had spent a few years in the military. He'd been injured several times. Been knocked unconscious twice. He knew what it was like to open your eyes and be disoriented. It was a hollow, lonely feeling. He'd recognized that lost feeling in her eyes. He'd been relatively fortunate with his own injuries, and his disorientation hadn't lasted for long. He hoped the same was true for her.

He pulled out his phone and punched in the number for a deputy working the crime scene in the woods. "Any chance you've found a blue metal lockbox?" he asked when the deputy answered.

"No. Are we looking for one?"

"Apparently there was one in the cab of her truck, but it's gone now."

"I'll pass the word to keep an eye out for it."

"What have you found so far?" Luke asked.

"Bullet casings. Partial footprints. A tree branch with blood on it and a few strands of hair. It was lying on the ground, near the spot where Ms. Graham was found. Of course we're going to check to see if the blood and hair are a match for her or if they belong to someone else."

"She's been admitted to the hospital, so I'm going by there later this evening to check on her. Maybe she will have recovered some of her memory by then."

"Sounds good."

"I'll be back over there at the crime scene in a few minutes."

Luke disconnected and turned to Peter. "Is there anything else you can think of to tell me?"

Peter cleared his throat. "No, sir."

The kid was still pretty pale and his hands were trembling. After ten years in the military, including several tours of combat, and his time as a deputy sheriff, it was hard for Luke to imagine how he would have reacted at the age of eighteen to having his employer attacked while he was just a short distance away.

He'd played football in high school and grew up on a ranch, so when he was eighteen he'd thought he was tough. But he wasn't. Witnessing how inhumanely people could treat each other was shocking. You had to learn how to keep your emotional distance so you could be useful at your job. So you stopped being shocked by brutality. Or told yourself that was the case, anyway.

Luke's brother, Jake, had warned him on one of Luke's visits home on leave that he was getting too good at the emotional-distance thing. And after he'd moved back to Idaho to help Jake with his kids, Luke had tried to work on that. Leaving the Army after his enlistment period ended was a tough decision. But it was one he'd had to make, because he'd had no idea how long his brother would need his help.

"How are you holding up?" he asked Peter. "You've been a lot of help, and I appreciate it. Do you need me to have a deputy drive you home?"

"No, sir. I called a friend to come pick me up and he's waiting in the parking lot."

After Peter left, Luke wrapped things up with Don and went back to the crime scene to see how the investigation was going. The perpetrator hadn't been found, but he'd left a trail through the woods that looped back to the two-lane highway winding through this part of the county. The guy could be anywhere by now.

If Melanie could eventually remember what the perpetrator looked like, there was the slim chance they could find an image of him on video. And from there, maybe link him to a vehicle license plate. A purchase made with a credit card at the fairgrounds. Something.

Confident that everything was being properly taken care of at the crime scene, Luke headed for the hospital. He arrived just as visiting hours were ending. When he stepped into Melanie's room, he was immediately greeted by a young red-haired woman who introduced herself as Melanie's cousin, Anna.

"How is she doing?" Luke asked Anna in a quiet voice. He could see Melanie lying in bed, a blanket pulled up nearly to her chin, looking tired and groggy.

"She has a concussion," Anna told him. "But no fractures. And no gunshot wounds."

"Thank You, Lord," Luke said softly.

"Amen," Anna agreed. "They've given her some painkillers and a sedative so she'll sleep."

"Has she regained any of her memory?"

Anna shook her head. "She still doesn't remember anything since she left Wyoming two weeks ago."

Melanie's eyelids fluttered open and she called out to Luke. "Hey, deputy."

Luke walked over to her. "How are you feeling?"

"Sleepy." She had bandages on one side of her head, and dark circles under her eyes. "Thank you," she mumbled, giving him a half smile. "And please thank the event security man who found me." Her smile started to falter and tears formed in the corners of her eyes. "Something happened to me," she said, with confusion evident in her eyes. She reached her hand up to touch the bandages on her head and gave him a pleading look. "What happened to me?"

"I'm going to do my best to find out."

Over the intercom, a voice announced the end of visiting hours.

"I'll talk to you again later," Luke said to Melanie as he headed for the door. And then to Anna, he said, "Can I speak with you for a minute?"

She followed him out into the hallway, calling back to Melanie that she wasn't actually leaving for the night just yet.

"Do you have any theories on who might have attacked her?" Luke asked. "Does she have an angry business partner? Maybe a boyfriend she broke up with?"

"She has an ex-husband, Ben," Anna said. "But he was the one who insisted on the divorce—told her he wanted to start a new life without her—so I wouldn't suspect him. I really can't think of anyone."

Luke glanced up and down the hallway, frustrated that he had no idea what the perpetrator looked like. "Do you know how long she'll be in the hospital?"

"There's a good chance she'll be able to leave tomorrow morning."

"Do the doctors have any idea how long it will take for her to regain her memory?"

"They said it could happen as early as tomorrow morning. Or it could take a few weeks." Anna's eyes teared up. She looked away and blinked rapidly. "Or the memories of the past two weeks might be gone forever. So she'd never be able to remember who attacked her, and that *criminal* would get away with it."

Luke sighed. He could not let that happen.

"When you get home try to relax as much as you can," the doctor said to Melanie as she tapped the information for Melanie's prescription into an electronic tablet. "You need to heal from the emotional trauma, as well as the physical injury. So don't try to force yourself to remember things. Otherwise you could end up right back here in the hospital again." The doctor's smile was kind, but she also managed to make it clear that she wasn't kidding.

Melanie remembered waking up in the woods last night. But prior to that, she still only remembered going to bed at the hotel in Wyoming. *Not* trying to remember what happened during those missing two weeks was difficult. Like trying not to scratch an itch.

The doctor left and Melanie turned to Anna. "All right, cousin. Let's roll." Hospital protocol required Melanie to sit in a wheelchair and be pushed out to the parking lot, even though she felt like she could walk.

"I need you to take me back to the fairgrounds, to get my truck and the trailer,"

Melanie said as soon as they were in Anna's sedan.

Anna turned to her with a cheery smile. "No." Despite the upbeat tone, Melanie could see the dark circles under her cousin's eyes, and the paleness of her skin made the freckles scattered across her face stand out even more defiantly.

Melanie wasn't the only one suffering in the aftermath of this bizarre attack on her. Anna had already done so much for her. And she had a husband, Tyler, serving in the military, overseas. Anna had enough weight on her shoulders. She didn't need anything added to that.

"That deputy said your truck and trailer are securely stored at the fairgrounds," Anna added as she turned the key and fired up the car's engine. "The smart thing for you to do is to go back to the house and unwind. We'll get your stuff later."

"Fine." Actually, going back to Anna's restored Victorian house, where Melanie rented a couple of rooms, one to use as a bedroom and the other for an office, sounded like a good idea. Closing the shades, lying in her bed and hiding from the world sounded like a *great* idea. Maybe she could numb her brain with mindless TV, as well. Because, although she was trying very hard to stay upbeat around Anna, her thoughts wanted to drift to some very dark places.

Someone had tried to *kill* her. Apparently for money. She had come in contact with someone evil. How was it possible someone could be like that? And how safe was anyone, ever, when there were people like that in the world?

Melanie began to tremble. A cold black wave of fear crashed over her, seemingly from out of nowhere. She couldn't catch her breath, and she quickly rolled down her window for some fresh air.

Anna glanced over at her. "You all right?"

"Coffee," Melanie said hoarsely. "Coffee would make me feel better."

"Sure."

Anna made the turn to take them to their favorite coffee shop. Melanie flipped down the sun visor and caught a glimpse of herself in the mirror. Pale. Bruised. Looking like someone who'd been attacked.

The trembling got worse, and the midsize sedan suddenly seemed way too small. Melanie wanted to get out of the car. She wanted to jump up. She wanted to run. She needed to *get away*. It didn't matter that she didn't know why.

The coffee shop didn't have a drive-through. Anna pulled into a parking space behind it, near the back entrance, and Melanie threw open her door before the car was completely stopped.

Anna gave her a questioning look.

"I'll take my usual," Melanie said to her. She gestured toward the front of the store, where there was a strip of grass and a couple of picnic tables. "Let's drink our coffee while we sit outside. In the sunshine. I'll meet you over there."

Hiding in her bedroom seemed like a horrible idea now. She needed to be outside, where she could move. Where she could run. For a split second she had a flash of memory. Of being chased in the woods.

The coffee shop was in an area with both businesses and residences. Moving down the alley, Melanie could see into people's backyards. See the houses, where normal life was going on. Where people felt safe.

Suddenly someone threw something over Melanie from behind her. A thick, heavy dark cloth that covered her head and shoulders and arms, down to her elbows. Before she could react, they wrenched it tight, pinning her arms to her sides, forcing the air out of her lungs. Then they started dragging her backward.

She tried to scream, but the cloth was tight across her mouth and she couldn't get enough air. Terror and panic set her heart racing. She fought again for a deep breath, but the cloth was pulled even tighter across her mouth.

The world began to spin. The sounds around her were muffled, but she could hear a dog barking. She started to feel strangely detached from everything that was happening around her. After that, there was nothing.

TWO

"The guy who lives in the house next to the coffee shop, Jon Stoker, called the cops to report the attack on you," Luke said to Melanie. "His dog wouldn't stop barking. He came out to see what the problem was and saw someone with a blanket pulled over your head, dragging you across the parking lot."

Melanie touched her fingertips to her lower lip, grateful to be alive and appreciating more than ever the ability to take a deep breath.

"When Mr. Stoker saw what was happening, he yelled and the person dragging you let go of the blanket and ran. Mr. Stoker hurried into his house for his phone and then came back outside while he called 9-1-1. He heard the roar of some kind of vehicle driving off, but he couldn't actually see it."

Melanie had apparently regained consciousness right after the attacker had let go of her. Anna had heard the commotion and hurried outside. She had pulled the blanket off Melanie just as Melanie was opening her eyes.

"The Bowen city police have been out, patrolling the neighborhood and going door-to-door, looking for anybody who witnessed anything. They also talked to customers and employees inside the coffee shop."

Melanie, Luke and Anna were sitting in the front parlor of Anna's house. Both Melanie and Anna loved vintage clothes, jewelry and home furnishings. The heavy furniture, thick curtains tied back with knotted silk tassels, crocheted doilies on the table tops and richly colored rugs on the hardwood floor gave Melanie a familiar feeling of stability and comfort. Something she desperately needed right now.

Luke had called ahead to ask if he could visit with Melanie for a few minutes. He'd arrived a short time ago, and Anna had invited him in and offered him tea, which he'd politely declined.

Luke sat in an upholstered club chair, with his sheriff's-department-issued cowboy hat in hand, leaning forward a little as though he were already anxious to leave. Melanie was across from him, seated at the end of a couch, clutching the couch's arm so tightly, her right hand was nearly numb. But she didn't care. It was something solid. And right now there wasn't much in her life that felt solid. Instead everything seemed disturbingly dreamlike. Normal life felt like something that had vanished a thousand years ago.

Anna sat close to her in a rocking chair.

"Did you go back to the hospital and get

checked out by the doctor after this second attack?" Luke asked.

Melanie started to nod. Pain made her stop. Her neck was stiff after being grabbed and dragged in the alley, and she had a pounding headache again. Those pains didn't mix well with the slight wave of dizziness that had come and gone, repeatedly, since she woke up this morning. For the moment it seemed best to stay as still as possible.

"I did see a doctor," she answered. "I have no new injuries, other than a sore neck." And a sense of impending panic that had started as soon as she had left the hospital, and it was apparently going to hang around for a while.

"This time I had nothing for anyone to steal," she said to the large lawman sitting across from her. "I didn't have my purse. I left it in the car. I wasn't even wearing any of my jewelry. They made me take it off when I arrived at the hospital, and I put it in my purse." Not that it was extremely valuable.

She wore what she made. She'd splurged and made a few pieces using gold, but the vast majority of her jewelry was made of silver and semiprecious stones. She couldn't afford anything more elaborate.

"This wasn't a robbery," Melanie said, with her voice sounding scratchy and tears forming in the corners of her eyes. "So, why is this happening to me?"

"I don't know. But I intend to find out." Luke cleared his throat. "Tell me what was in the lockbox," he said. "Maybe that has something to do with all of this."

Melanie blinked several times, trying to figure out what he was talking about. "What lockbox?"

"Peter told me you had a blue lockbox with you, all three days of the rodeo, and that it was with you in the truck when he saw you just before the attack at the fairgrounds. After that it was missing. It hasn't turned up yet."

Melanie stared at him, trying hard to remember her time at the rodeo, here in Miles County. But her efforts brought her straight to a blank wall. And the harder she tried to remember, the closer she got to that feeling of panic. "I can't remember," she whispered, afraid that if she spoke normally, she'd burst into tears or scream.

"You have that beige metal box you've used as a cashbox for a while," Anna said. "Where is it?"

Melanie glanced at her cousin. "You can't seriously be asking me that," she said. "I don't know where *I've* been for the last two weeks. How could I possibly know where that box is?" She started to shake her head and stopped when the pain started. "I don't even know where the items I had left over at the end of the rodeo are."

"Your trailer is still locked," Luke said. "I haven't seen inside it. But I have seen inside your truck. There are several clear storage boxes stacked in the back seat. Looks like your jewelry is in there."

"I'm glad to hear it," Melanie said. At least that was one less thing to worry about.

"I can drive your truck and trailer back here," Luke said. "Or wherever you'd like me to take them. You live here, correct?"

"Yes." Melanie glanced at Anna, feeling bad for having just snapped at her. "I've lived here for the last year."

Luke turned to Anna. "So, you know for certain that Melanie has been in town for the last two weeks, even though she doesn't remember it?"

"Yes." Anna nodded. "You came straight back here after your trip to Wyoming," she said, directing the rest of her response to Melanie. "You arrived on time. You were happy. You'd sold some jewelry and that oak-dresser-and-nightstand set you'd restored. The one you bought from the Wilsons."

"I remember that," Melanie said, feeling like recalling it was some kind of triumph. "I remember arriving in Leopold early and going to the big flea market in the parking lot outside the rodeo, looking for things I could buy and fix up and then resell. I remember getting my booth set up inside the rodeo grounds and talking to customers. And I remember selling that oak-dresser-and-nightstand set to a newlywed couple." Why was it that she could remember being at the rodeo in Wyoming, remember making that sale, remember packing up when it was all over and then…nothing?

"Stop it," her cousin commanded in a kind tone. Anna glanced at Luke. "Her doctor told her not to try too hard to remember that missing stretch of time and risk getting herself upset. She's supposed to relax and let her mind and body heal."

"I'd like to see *you* relax after going through what I've been through," Melanie grumbled. "I just think something must have happened after I packed up in Wyoming. Otherwise, why does my memory end there?"

"The doctor said recent memories sometimes disappear after a head injury like yours," Anna said. "That trip was recent. Doesn't mean anything significant happened there. And the doctor said there's a good chance your memory will come back."

Anna turned to Luke. "If you look at the security video from the bank and from several different stores in town, you'll see she was here. And we can find plenty of witnesses if we need to." She looked at Melanie. "You've got a hard head. Getting hit by a tree branch couldn't have done that much damage. You'll be fine. Give it time."

Despite feeling miserable, Melanie mustered a slight smile. She didn't have much family living around Bowen anymore, just a couple of cousins on her mother's side and her dad's widower uncle, and sometimes that bothered her. But the family she did have always came through in a pinch. Then she glanced down at her hands. They had scrapes all over them. She swallowed thickly. "Why do you think the guy who attacked me today didn't just shoot me?" she asked Luke. "Apparently shooting me wasn't a problem for him last night."

"I don't know. My best guess would be that he was afraid of witnesses. It was broad daylight. In the center of town. The sound of gunshots would have drawn a lot of attention."

The doorbell chimed and Melanie's heart sank. It could be some kind soul coming by to check up on her. And with her emotions all over the place and her strength fading, she wasn't sure how polite she could be.

Luke got to his feet. "You expecting anyone?"

"No," Anna said, walking to the door. Luke followed behind her. She pulled aside the narrow gauze curtain covering the strip of glass beside the door and looked out. "It's a police officer," she said.

It was a patrol officer stopping by to deliver the message that the chief of police wanted to make certain Melanie understood the police department would be working with the sheriff's department to find the person who'd attacked her. Since the first attack took place in county jurisdiction, the sheriff's department was taking the lead in the investigation. "But then I guess you already knew all this," the officer said, glancing at Luke. "Since Lieutenant Baxter is officially in charge of your case."

No, Melanie hadn't known that. She glanced at Luke and he gave her a slight nod. From what she'd seen so far, the lieutenant was capable and compassionate. Despite the seriousness of the situation, she felt a flutter of attraction and the whisper of some deeper emotion in the center of her chest. Was it possible he'd had himself put in charge of her case because he felt something like that, too?

The officer didn't stay long. As soon as he left, Anna ran upstairs to Melanie's office to look for her beige lockbox. She came back a few minutes later, carrying it. There was a big dent in it, and as soon as Melanie saw it, she remembered dropping it in the parking lot behind The Mercantile.

"That's right. It got dented and I remember buying the new blue one," Melanie said to Luke, thrilled at the inkling of memory. "But I planned to use it the same way I did the old one. I didn't keep drugs or secret government files or anything else you might be imagining in there. Just money. Not even very much, really. And a little jewelry." Yet someone tried to take her life over that. It was hard to fathom.

Luke nodded and got to his feet.

He glanced around. "I don't see any signs of a security system for the house," he said. "I'd strongly suggest you invest in one. The police will patrol by here as often as they can," he added. "Make sure you keep your doors and windows locked."

A look of panic flashed across Anna's face. "Let me check the back doors," she said, heading for the kitchen.

Melanie stood up and walked with Luke to the front door.

"Tell me something," she said, her words stopping him before he opened the door. "Both attacks must be related. Why do you think the guy came after me a second time?"

He hesitated, obviously thinking over his answer before he spoke. "Well, since he shot at you, it could be argued that the initial attack was attempted murder and not simply a robbery. And that could mean a pretty lengthy prison sentence. He'd have no way of knowing you were having trouble with your memory and couldn't identify him. So maybe he came after you because he was afraid you'd identify him and send him to prison."

"But that seems irrational. Even if I could recognize his face, what are the odds I'd ever see the guy again?"

"Apparently he thought the odds were pretty good," Luke said. "Which makes me think he is someone you know."

Luke stepped outside. Melanie closed and locked the door behind him. All the while a chill passed through her. Was it really possible someone she'd known had attacked her *twice*?

"Uncle Luke, come out here! Billy Clyde is in the mud again!"

Luke stood inside the stables at his family's ranch. At the sound of his five-year-old niece Kayla's voice, he turned toward the big open door to look at her standing in the sunlight. "Come on!" She waved impatiently at him.

Luke finished drying his hands on a tattered red shop towel and walked outside. His niece was already running ahead of him. She stopped and called out "Billy Clyde!" while slapping her thigh.

Billy Clyde, a scruffy brown-and-black dog of uncertain breed, was happily rolling in something on the ground in the corral. A couple of horses had been in that corral until an hour ago. Luke was fairly certain it wasn't mud the dog was rolling in. And he was doing it right after they'd given Billy Clyde a bath.

"Billy Clyde!" Jake Baxter, Luke's younger brother, walked from the ranch house, down the slight hill, and hollered to his dog. "Billy Clyde, come here!"

The dog paused, looked at him, then went right back to rolling around.

"I think that dog's going deaf," Jake said when he got up alongside Luke.

"There's nothing wrong with him," Luke said as both men watched Kayla and her seven-year-old brother, Alan, race over to the dog. At their approach, Billy Clyde jumped up and started barking and playfully running away from them. "That dog's getting up in years and he's going to do what he wants to do," Luke added.

"He's always done what he wanted to do," Jake muttered. "When he first showed up, he was skin and bones. Limping. Patches of his fur missing. Janelle felt sorry for him and spoiled him rotten. *That* is the true source of the problem with Billy Clyde."

Luke glanced over at Jake, relieved to see that his brother could mention his late wife's name without choking up. Jake and Janelle had married right out of high school. They had settled here, at the family ranch, while Luke joined the army and took off to see the world. Luke had come back to visit when he could. And, of course, when their father had died. Their mother had passed away when they were both young.

Luke had been energized by the adrenaline rush of serving in the military. Couldn't imagine ever coming back and settling for a quiet ranch life, just a few miles outside of Bowen.

But then his sister-in-law had started to get sick. The end had come so swiftly for her that Luke was truly at a loss for words when he got the news while on an army base in Afghanistan. Even for a man who had faced the horrors of combat daily, when the phone call came, telling him that his upbeat, fun-loving sister-in-law was gone, he'd had a hard time believing it.

And his little brother had been a wreck. Not only had Jake faced the horror of losing his wife, but he knew from experience the feeling of emptiness left behind when children lose their mother at an early age. And worry for those kids started eating him up.

Eventually Jake pulled himself together. Kept putting one foot in front of the other, because he was tough. Always had been. He didn't complain, but Luke had heard the heaviness in his brother's voice when he talked to him. And he knew what he had to do.

Luke had been near the end of his tour of duty when Janelle had passed away. He hadn't reenlisted yet, though up to that point he'd had every intention of doing so. Instead he finished his tour and came on home and moved to the ranch to help his brother. Not so much with managing the ranch. Jake had a handle on that. But with raising the kids. With getting on with life.

That had been two years ago. Being a Miles County deputy sheriff was a long way from the intense challenges Luke was used to facing on a daily basis. But once the kids were a little older, and he was convinced Jake was emotionally settled, Luke would get back to traveling the world. Seeing new things. Facing new challenges. Maybe he'd reenlist in the military. Or see what was available in the world of private security.

His thoughts drifted to Melanie Graham. He'd responded to assaults and strong-arm robberies before, but her case was certainly unique. One of the most interesting cases he'd worked in a while.

It was because of the amnesia angle, and the second attack taking place so soon after the first, that he'd made sure the sheriff's department pushed to be the lead agency on the case. And he'd made certain he was put in charge of the investigation.

He found himself recalling Melanie Graham's face. The fear and confusion in her eyes. He'd seen that so many times in combat. He couldn't stand by and let somebody go through that without helping them. And okay, maybe he was a little motivated to help Melanie specifically. In just the small amount of time he'd spent around her, he'd been drawn in by the appeal of her strength and determination to work through the aftermath of the attack on her rather than remaining paralyzed by fear. Her warm hazel eyes and defiant smile, at moments when he knew she was afraid, had their appeal, as well. The woman was a fighter.

Luke wrenched himself back to the present and glanced around. Billy Clyde had let the kids catch him and they were rolling around in the thick grass outside the corral together.

"Little brother," Luke said, turning and

clapping Jake on the shoulder. "You are going to have to give both of your kids a bath tonight."

"Tonight and every night," Jake said agreeably. "Sometimes in the middle of the day, too."

"I'll give Billy Clyde another bath. Unless you want to make him stay outside tonight."

Jake laughed and shook his head. "I can't make that animal stay outside and he knows it." Then, just like a cloud passing over the sun on a clear day, his expression completely changed. He cleared his throat a couple of times. "Janelle insisted we keep him after he showed up that day, and he was always really her dog. Maybe that's why he's always acting up. Maybe he misses her, too."

Jake's voice broke and he dragged his knuckles across his eyes, wiping away the tears that had slipped out.

Luke stood by him. As usual he was clueless about what he should say. But he knew there was power in having someone present when you were hurting. Even if they didn't say a word.

By the time the smelly dog and the kids ran over to them, Jake had composed himself. "I'm starving," Alan announced.

"Yeah, well, the way you two smell, it's going to be baths first and then supper," Jake answered.

The three of them turned and started up the hill to the house.

Luke headed back to the stables with the dog at his heels so he could fill the big tub in there with soapy water and re-bathe Billy Clyde.

"I still can't remember what happened to me at the fairgrounds," Melanie said to Luke, with exasperation burning in her chest like indigestion. "How do you expect me to identify the attacker in these pictures?"

Two days had passed since she'd been grabbed in the alley beside the coffee shop.

Three days since someone had tried to kill her at the fairgrounds.

Physically and emotionally she'd taken a slight turn for the worse, once she was settled in her room at her cousin's house, after the second attack.

Every time she let down her defenses, told herself to relax and tried to get some sleep, that panicky feeling would come back with a vengeance. Her neck hurt even more, as did the scrapes and bruises on the places where she'd hit the ground. She was afraid to take the sleeping pills and painkillers the doctor had prescribed for her. Because what if the attacker came back again? Tried to break into the house?

She was doing a little better now. Well enough to drive herself to the sheriff's department's office in town and meet with Luke to look at mug shots. Anna had offered to take her to the meeting, but she'd already missed enough work looking after Melanie. And it was a short drive. Melanie could handle it. Like so many things these days, she *had* to handle it.

When Melanie's husband had filed for divorce, she'd needed somewhere to go. Anna had welcomed her with open arms. The rent money Melanie paid was appreciated. Anna made that abundantly clear. But Anna still needed to show up at the accounting firm where she'd recently gotten a job. And thanks to Melanie, she'd already missed two days of work.

Luke took a sip of coffee and set the mug on the conference table, where they were seated. There was an electronic tablet in front of him and he slid it over toward her. "These are pictures of men from this part of Idaho, as well as a few from Northern Wyoming who have a history of violent, strong-arm robbery, specifically targeting women." The screen showed four images. She could swipe her finger across the screen to see more.

"Do me a favor and just take a look," he

continued. "See if anyone seems familiar. It's possible you crossed paths with the attacker more than two weeks ago and that you'd remember him if you saw his picture. Maybe he worked alongside you at a rodeo or a fair or somewhere else where you were selling your jewelry over the last few months."

That was possible. She'd been busy over the summer, traveling to as many events as she could.

"Or maybe he's someone who's seen you working at The Mercantile," he added.

The Mercantile was a former general store in Bowen that had been renovated and turned into a crafts-and-antiques mini mall. Melanie rented space in the communal area, at the center of the store.

"Maybe someone got the idea to rob you after seeing you put money into that blue lockbox that's missing. Or maybe they saw you put those few pieces of gold jewelry you've said you made into the box. Or perhaps something else," he added, with his eyebrows slightly raised and a questioning expression on his face.

She didn't like his tone when he said the words "something else," and she turned to frown at him. Maybe she shouldn't care so much that he was questioning her character, but she did. Probably because she'd felt a connection, like friendship, forming between them. And that made his comment strike deeper than it would have if it had come from somebody else. "If you think I had drugs or something stolen or illegal in that box, you're mistaken," she said icily. "I may not remember that box or specifically what's in it at the moment, but I do know who I am."

He held her gaze for several seconds and then finally nodded, though she didn't think he looked convinced.

She knew he was a cop. People probably lied to him all of the time. He saw the worst of society. But that didn't lessen the sting of his suspicion.

She picked up the tablet. Swiped her finger across the screen to turn the pages. It took a while, but she finally got to the end. No one looked familiar.

She glanced up at him, shook her head and found herself blinking back tears. It had been irrational for her to get her hopes up. To think she might somehow recognize the perpetrator in these pictures and bring this nightmare to an end.

Haven't I been through enough? She thought of her husband's betrayal and insistence on ending their six-year marriage. And the financial bottoming-out that followed the divorce. Now there were these attacks. It was too much.

She immediately felt ashamed of herself for giving in to self-pity. People suffered through a lot worse. *Whatever is good and noble, think on those things.* Clearly that was what she needed to be doing.

"Looking at mug shots is not our only strategy in this investigation," Luke said. "It's just one idea."

Melanie nodded. "I'm willing to help any way I can."

Luke reached for the tablet and she slid it toward him. "So, how are you doing?" he asked. Melanie started to fib, telling him she was fine. But then she thought about the promise she'd made to herself after being blindsided by her husband. *Ex*-husband. There was a lot Ben had kept secret. Including his relationship with the woman he'd begun seeing while he was still married to Melanie.

She should have seen it coming, she'd told herself. But how could she? In so many ways, she and Ben had barely known each other. They'd gotten married straight out of high school, moved to California, found jobs and started living their lives together.

Yet in so many important ways, they'd always been strangers. She just hadn't realized it until the divorce papers were sitting on her dining room table, ready for her signature.

She couldn't control other people—she accepted that—but she could control herself. She could keep the promise she'd made to herself to be open and forthcoming. And it was reasonable to expect the same thing from anyone she had a relationship with.

Not that she had a relationship with Lieutenant Baxter. Maybe the feelings she'd thought they were beginning to share were all on her part. Maybe she was reading something into the situation between them that wasn't there, because she was afraid and feeling alone. In any event, being transparent was a standard she was setting for herself. So she would tell him the truth.

"My head and neck, and everywhere else I've been injured, have hurt for the last couple of days, but it's better now," she finally blurted out in answer to his question. "I'm still jumpy, though. I can't relax. And I'm scared."

And then, even though it made her horribly uncomfortable, she looked him in the eyes and waited for his reaction.

"I'm not surprised," he said. "You've been through two traumatic experiences in less than twenty-four hours." He glanced down at his phone screen and she thought that was the end of it.

But then he turned back to her, and looking slightly uncomfortable, he said, "My experience is that it takes a lot longer to work through the aftermath of a violent attack than you'd think. But if you hang on, and ask for help if you need it, you'll be okay."

"Right." He hadn't given her any advice that would make her problems disappear in an instant like she wanted them to. But the empathy he was expressing felt sincere. And the honest assessment that it would take a while for things to heal was probably something she'd needed to hear to make her expectations more realistic.

"Do you want me to help you get your

truck and trailer to the house this afternoon?" he asked.

"I think the trip here is all I can handle today." There was no reason for her to feel physically exhausted, yet she did. And that panicky feeling was starting to come back. Not as severely as it had felt before, but still it was there. She needed to get home before it got worse.

"Can we get them tomorrow?" she asked.

"Of course."

They both stood at the same time. Her knees were shaky and she reached her hand out to the conference table to steady herself. Luke reached out and held on to her lower arm, keeping her from toppling over. His big, calm presence made her feel stronger. His touch sent a *zing* through her that she wished she could ignore.

"Thank you," she said after a moment, and he released her arm.

"I'll walk you out to your car," he said. "I

need to get out of the building and do some patrolling, anyway."

She'd come in the small sedan she kept for driving around town. Her truck was a gas-guzzler. Once she was inside the car, with the doors locked, she waved at Luke and he walked over to his truck.

Anxious to get back to the house where she hoped to rest and relax, Melanie started up the engine and then pulled out of the parking lot, onto the street.

In the rearview mirror she could see that Luke followed her all the way home. It felt reassuring to know he was there. And comforting to know that a man like Luke was looking out for her.

THREE

"Are you sure it's safe for you to be here?" Diana Wooldridge, owner of The Mercantile, shoved up the gray sleeves of her sweater, frowned at Melanie and then crossed her arms.

"I'm as safe here as I would be sitting at home," Melanie answered. That might not be exactly true. But she felt more nervous sitting at home alone. At least here she had people around her. "And I want to take a look over my inventory. Has anything sold while I've been away?"

"A few things. Come on back." Diana tilted her head toward her office. "Let me take a look at my sales reports."

They walked by displays of handmade

soaps and scented candles, area rugs and stained glass, knitted sweaters and whimsical wooden birdfeeders. On their way they passed by two of Diana's employees, who were working with customers at the sales counter, and each one gave Melanie a sympathetic smile when they saw her.

Most of the town must know what had happened by now. She was still getting so many calls from concerned friends offering support and nosey acquaintances looking for juicy gossip that she'd finally silenced the ringer on her phone this morning.

She'd had a rough night and her nerves felt stretched tight.

Every night since the attack, she'd woken from nightmares, though she couldn't remember exactly what she'd been dreaming. Last night she'd woken up twice, and each time she'd remembered a bit of the nightmare that woke her. In the first dream someone was behind her, telling her that her life was over, and the feeling of sorrow was so deep that she'd woken up crying.

The second dream was a vague sense of herself running through dark woods, desperately trying to escape an invisible source of terror.

Were they just dreams? Or were they the beginnings of her memory coming back? And if a dream could be that scary, how terrifying might the actual memories be?

Maybe not remembering was a blessing.

As she walked down the short hallway to Diana's office, her gaze fell on a bright red, white and blue poster thumbtacked to the wall, which read Dwayne Skinner Presents the Magnificent Miles County Rodeo. Mr. Skinner had brought by several of those posters a month ago. And once again he'd good-naturedly badgered Melanie to go into business with him.

A former rodeo champion at the national level, Mr. Skinner was now an events promoter, as well as the owner of several other businesses. He did a lot for the community, and he'd become a familiar face through his advertisements on TV, social media and even billboards, down on the interstate. It was flattering that he was impressed enough with her business to consider working with her, and he certainly had a lot of money to invest and help her business grow, but doing it all on her own was important to her.

After all of those times she'd walked past that poster, thinking about the things she would bring to try to sell at the rodeo, never ever had it crossed her mind that something bad would happen to her there.

She shivered as she walked down the hallway. Partly because the building was old and drafty, and partly because she couldn't help thinking about how close she'd come to the end of her life.

Up ahead, from Diana's office, she heard the sound of Peter's voice.

When she stepped inside the office, Diana was getting seated in her desk chair. She clicked on her computer mouse and looked at the screen of her laptop. Peter sat at a table with a microwave and a coffeepot. He had a bag of bread in front of him and a jar of peanut butter open beside it. He was chewing hard on what appeared to be a very sticky sandwich.

He worked at The Mercantile when Diana could use him, and for Melanie when she had the occasional sales event at some other location. He was a reliable, hardworking young man.

"How are you doing?" Peter managed to say after taking a big gulp of water. Melanie had practically been able to see the lump of bread and peanut butter travel down his skinny throat.

"I'm all right," she said, not wanting to lie to him, but not wanting to place her emotional burdens on him, either.

"While you were down in Wyoming, we sold seven pairs of your earrings, four necklaces and one of the antique lamps you rewired," Diana said. She turned from the screen to glance at Melanie. "You have a talent for making what people want."

The sound of footsteps walking down the short hallway, toward the office, sent a wave of panic flooding through Melanie's body. Before she could even think about what she was doing, she found herself on the opposite side of the office, with her back pressed up against Diana's old wooden file cabinet. Its brass handles pressed hard against Melanie's spine. Her heart beat so rapidly in her chest, it felt like it could lift up into her throat at any second.

Luke stepped across the threshold, the expression on his face determined, and his gaze quickly scanning the office until it settled on Melanie. A warm ripple of relief passed through her body when she recognized it was him. Followed by a flutter of nerves in the pit of her stomach. From her reckoning, the atmosphere in the room had gone from fearful to electrically charged by his presence, in the blink of an eye.

"You all right?" he asked.

"Of course," she answered, the squeaky sound of her voice betraying the jangle of emotions she couldn't quite sort out at the moment.

Luke kept staring at her. And then she realized Diana and Peter were also staring at her.

Embarrassment turned the skin of her cheeks warm. She forced in another breath, loosened the fists she didn't realize she'd made with her hands and stepped forward from the file cabinet. "I'm okay," she said, managing to make her voice sound normal this time. "I don't know what's wrong with me."

Luke finally stopped staring at her. He pulled off the cowboy hat that was part of his deputy sheriff's uniform and glanced around the office, his stance visibly relaxing. "I'm just glad you're safe."

A sense of alarm raced up her spine. "Why wouldn't I be safe? What happened?"

"I called you and you didn't answer. I was concerned, so I went by the house, but no one was there. Your neighbor, Sheila, saw me. She told me you were probably here."

Melanie walked over to the purse she'd dropped in a chair, pulled out her phone and saw that she had several missed calls and texts.

"I'm sorry," she said. "I turned off the ringer and meant to turn it back on before I left the house. I just needed a break."

"Right now taking a break from your phone is a bad idea," Luke said flatly. "Keep the ringer turned on."

While his opinion was likely right, she didn't care for being spoken to that way. She wasn't reckless. She was just tired. Her nerves were frayed. And she was obviously very jumpy. "Why did you want to get ahold of me?" she asked.

"We found your lockbox," he said. "In the

woods, about a half mile south of where we found you."

She glanced at his hands. He hadn't brought it with him. "I take it the thing was broken into a million pieces."

"It's in my truck," he said. "I'll be right back."

The box did look vaguely familiar when Luke returned with it a few minutes later. And after giving it a little bit of thought, Melanie remembered shopping for lockboxes online.

"I assume it's empty," she said.

"As a matter of fact, it's not." He set it on the table.

Peter watched what was happening, looking fascinated. Diana was likewise paying close attention, perched on the edge of her office chair.

Melanie had noticed a small set of unfamiliar keys in a zippered compartment in her purse. She'd guessed now that this box was what they were for and she retrieved them. She slipped a key into the lock, turned it and lifted the lid.

"How can that be?" she said, looking down at the contents. "I don't understand."

She was looking at cash. At least six hundred dollars, she would guess. Plus three small jewelry boxes. She opened them, and each one contained a pair of earrings made of gold. The expensive ones that she kept an especially close eye on. She looked up at Luke. "If somebody robbed me, why didn't he take this with him?"

Luke looked down at the open box. "It's possible the guy panicked, maybe he thought he was about to get caught and he tossed it so he could run faster."

Melanie thought of her nightmares. Unfortunately trying harder to remember her dreams didn't make them, or her memories, any clearer.

"Another possibility," Luke added, "is that he only wanted it to look like a robbery that had taken a violent turn. Maybe his real goal from the beginning was to kill you."

The room seemed to tilt a bit and Melanie reached back to the filing cabinet to steady herself. She wasn't one for dramatic scenes. The feeling that she was on the verge of fainting was real. She blamed it on her head injury.

"Do you still want to go to the fairgrounds and get your truck and trailer and bring them back to your house today?" Luke asked. "Or do you want to wait?"

He was watching her carefully. She thought she'd been subtle when she'd tried to catch her balance. But maybe not.

"I think I need to go home and rest right now," she answered. And the sooner she got there, the better. It seemed like any time she went anywhere or did anything, she was quickly exhausted. "Can we do it tomorrow?"

"I can have another deputy give me a hand and we can take care of it today for you."

"I'd rather wait and do it tomorrow," Melanie said. "I want to be there." Maybe being back at the fairgrounds would trigger her memory.

It was one thing if the jerk who'd attacked her had just wanted to rob her. That was a random event that could happen to anyone. But if he'd been intent on killing her, that was a completely different thing.

Luke walked with her downstairs and out of the store. He headed to his sheriff's department pickup truck. She headed to her car. Once again he followed her home. People didn't often list *reliability* as a romantic quality, but it was. Especially to a woman whose former husband could not be counted on—not when things got difficult. But Luke Baxter was not like that. She already knew she could count on him.

It was comforting to see him in her rearview mirror. But it was also chilling to know why he was following her. And that another attack could come at any time, from any direction.

* * *

"Did you grow up around here?" Melanie asked. "I grew up around here."

Luke turned the wheel of his sheriff's department pickup truck and entered the packed-dirt parking lot of the fairgrounds, feeling the rumble as they crossed over the cattle guard.

He knew nervous chatter when he heard it. She'd been talking nonstop since he'd picked her up at her house. He understood why she was on edge, and once again he'd offered to have someone else help him get her truck and trailer returned to her. But she'd refused.

"Yes, I grew up around here," he said. "On a horse ranch, near the northern edge of the county."

"So, you've lived here your whole life?" she continued as he drove up to the main building, where Don was going to meet them. It was a weekday; nothing much was going on except for a little grounds maintenance work. They were going to need someone to unlock a building so they could retrieve Melanie's truck and trailer.

If it were anybody else asking about his personal life, Luke would have redirected the conversation to something neutral, like horses or the weather. But he could tell she was trying hard to be brave. And he wanted to help her. For some reason, with Melanie, the temptation to share a little bit of himself was hard to resist.

"I left Idaho for a while," he said.

"Oh, me, too," she quickly interrupted him. "I got married right out of high school and we moved to California. Where did you go?"

He glanced over and she was literally wringing her hands, staring in the direction of the woods, where they'd found her.

"I went to a lot of places," he said. "All over the world. Mostly the Middle East. I was in the army."

She turned to him, with a questioning expression on her face that he'd seen numerous times after letting people know he was a combat veteran. She wanted to say something supportive, but she wasn't sure what he wanted to hear.

"It was the right decision for me for about ten years," he said. "Right now it feels good to be home. In a year or so I'll move on again."

"I lived just outside Los Angeles," she said while he put the truck in Park and texted Don to let him know they'd arrived. "I was there for about six years. My brother and parents moved to Seattle during that time. Most of my family lives over there now."

Family. Most of Luke's relatives lived in the southern end of the state. The army had been like a family to him. It still was. He might not be active duty anymore, but he stayed connected.

Maybe not connected enough. He realized there were a couple of his buddies he really missed. He hadn't talked to them in a while.

The old Luke would have shaken off the

feeling as something inconsequential. That's what he'd learned from his dad. A hard-working widower who'd done everything he could to provide for his boys. As the elder son, Luke had tried to be the same way.

Jake, on the other hand, had always been different. Probably more like their mom. And Luke had teased him about it until Jake had gotten married and had Alan and Kayla. Then he'd started thinking about how nice it must be to have your family surrounding you at the end of every day.

Apparently, though, that wasn't the kind of life Luke was wired for.

His phone chimed. It was a text from Don, saying he wasn't actually at the fairgrounds right now, but that someone would be out to meet them and get them access to the truck and trailer in just a minute.

Surprised at how far his thoughts had taken him, Luke glanced over at Melanie. That was what anything beyond surface conversation did to you. It got you thinking about things other than the job at hand. Remembering things you couldn't change. Feeling things. Maybe he'd try a little of the talking-and-feeling thing for the sake of his niece and nephew. But only for them. He had to draw the line somewhere.

"Can you remember anything about what happened here?" Luke asked quietly when he noticed Melanie was again staring in the direction where she'd been found.

She sighed. "Just being in Wyoming, and then waking up here and being found by the event security guy and then you. Those two missing weeks are still a blank." She shook her head slightly. "I've been dreaming a lot about things that are scary, but when I wake up I can't remember the details. I don't know if those are memories working their way to the surface or if they're just random dreams that don't mean anything."

Luke had no advice to offer her on that point. When he'd been knocked unconscious in combat and woken up confused about where he was and what had happened, he'd recovered his memory within a few hours. He had no experience with anything this long-term.

One of the doors to the fairgrounds' office building opened and a young woman with black braids and a boldly striped blue-and-green Western-style shirt came out to greet them. She took them to the events building, where she unlocked and opened a large roll-up door.

Luke and Melanie stepped inside. Melanie walked up to her truck, opened the driver's door and looked around. Luke stayed fairly close behind her, watching over her shoulder, curious to see if she was looking for anything specific.

He saw her gaze settle on smudges of black powder. "We dusted for fingerprints," he explained.

She reached into the back seat, picked up a laptop and looked at it. Then she went through a half dozen medium-sized storage boxes, which were also sitting on the back seat. There was no missing the glittering sight of silver jewelry in display trays.

She rifled through her purse for her key ring, then went around to the back of the small trailer and unfastened the lock. When she pulled open the door, Luke was right behind her again. Over her shoulder he could see small pieces of old furniture. Bookcases, end tables and a wooden frame for a child's bed. Some of the pieces were simply varnished or painted a solid color. Others had flowers or leafy vines painted on them.

She closed the door and replaced the lock. Luke could see that she was shaking. "Maybe we should wait a few minutes before you start driving," he suggested.

"I want to get out of here now," she said.

"I'll follow you home." He was spending a lot of time following her on the road, and that was fine with him. Protecting people was what he was paid to do. And with no suspects to chase down, no particularly useful evidence to pursue, there wasn't much he could do right now but keep an eye on her.

"I usually keep the trailer in a storage space," she said.

"Fine, I'll follow you to the storage facility."

She drove a little over the speed limit, but not by much. And Luke was happy to see she used the storage facility in town with video surveillance and an owner who lived on-site.

He waited nearby while she expertly backed the trailer into her storage building and locked the door. Luke politely refused to be baited into conversation by the facility owner, who wanted to gossip through Luke's truck window while Melanie was getting her stuff stowed.

He followed her back to the house and helped her carry her boxes of jewelry inside. When that was taken care of, she sighed heavily and told him she was going to make some very strong coffee and offered him a cup.

"Thank you, but I can't stay."

"Of course," she said. She walked him to the door.

He paused, with his hand resting on the door handle. "I've mentioned this before, but I want to ask you again, directly. Is there anything you're involved in that you aren't telling me about?" He had to know the truth if he was going to help her. And he had to know the truth for his own sake, before he got too caught up in thinking about her eyes and her smile. Before he let down his guard and told her too much about himself. "Have you gotten mixed up in something not exactly legal? Something that's put you on the wrong side of somebody dangerous?"

Her jaw muscles visibly tightened. The expression in her eyes went from friendly to shocked to outraged in just a few seconds. "You really think that's possible?" she asked, her voice barely above a whisper.

He raised an eyebrow. "Is it?"

"*No!*"

"None of us is perfect," he said. "And I'm obviously including myself. Nearly every day I come across someone who's in trouble because they've made a bad decision. Maybe because they were scared. Or broke. Or hopeless."

"Well, that's not the case with me."

"Okay. I'm glad to know that."

Luke stepped outside and she closed the door firmly behind him. He waited a few seconds, then called out, "Don't forget to lock it."

He heard the dead bolt snap loudly into place.

Maybe she was telling him the truth. Maybe she thought she was, but she'd actually gotten herself into some kind of trouble she didn't remember because of her head injury.

Either way it would be wise for Luke to tread carefully and keep his focus where it belonged: on capturing the assailant. Because he had to assume whoever had tried to kill Melanie once would try again.

It didn't matter what Miles County Deputy Sheriff Lieutenant Luke Baxter thought about her personally, Melanie told herself the next morning.

He was a cop doing his job, and they were supposed to be suspicious.

Really, it didn't matter what anyone thought of her. Not the town gossips who'd been full of opinions when she'd returned to Bowen after her divorce. Not her former husband, who'd told her she wasn't thin enough, wasn't social enough, wasn't fun-loving enough.

So what if she tended toward being a little chubby? If she enjoyed sipping coffee in the kitchen with a couple of close friends more than trying to impress people at a cocktail party? If she liked to have fun, but needed fun to be balanced with a feeling of accomplishment?

Melanie pulled her truck up to the entrance at the storage facility, punched her code into the security box and waited for the black gates to roll open.

After Luke had left the house yesterday, she'd felt like she'd chewed nails all afternoon, fuming over his accusation. When Anna came home from work, and Melanie told her what had happened, her cousin had pointed out that a question was not the same as an accusation. Melanie knew her reaction was out of proportion, but she couldn't help it.

The storage-facility gate rolled open, clanging loudly as it moved. She drove past it, to her storage space, and parked in front of the roll-up door.

"Hey! How you doing?" Sherman Webber, owner of the storage facility, was already standing by her truck door before she could even open it. A short, round, older gentleman with thick glasses and bad hearing, he considered it part of his job to talk to everybody who came onto the premises.

"Good morning," Melanie answered him.

Not everyone appreciated Sherman's nosiness, but Melanie didn't mind it. She figured there was a chance it actually did help keep her property more secure if Sherman was checking on everybody.

"You're here early!" Sherman said, sticking with his tendency to shout.

The eastern horizon was pale blue above the jagged mountaintops, but the sun wasn't quite up yet. From the direction of Sherman's office, she could hear the early news blaring on his TV.

"I need to get a lot done today," she told him. Bad dreams had woken her in the night; they were shadowy and vague, but frightening nevertheless. Finally, she'd just gotten up for the day and brewed some coffee. While sipping it, she'd thought over the events of the last few days.

She needed to cancel her remote sales

events for the next month. There was no way she was going to risk going out of town. She did not want to be on her own, and she was smart enough to appreciate the protection offered to her by Luke and local law enforcement if she stayed in Bowen. Hopefully whoever was attacking her would be caught soon. What made the most business sense would be to stock whatever she could fit into the floor space she rented at The Mercantile, and then inventory and photograph whatever was left over and try to sell it online.

"Heard you lost your memory!" Sherman shouted.

Oh, yeah, she lived in a small town. Everybody knew everything.

Melanie unlocked her storage-space door and rolled it up. "My head got hit pretty hard," she said. "But I think I'm healing up."

"You're young and strong," Sherman said, speaking loudly but not actually yelling at her this time. "You'll be fine. And I've got to say, there's some stuff I can't remember

anymore and I'm probably better off for it."
He laughed at his joke, obviously trying to
cheer her up.

She smiled at him. "You make a good
point."

"Well, I'll let you get to it." He gave her a
wave before turning and trundling back toward his office, bobbing slightly side to side
as he walked.

Melanie turned her attention back to her
storage space. She'd managed to pack quite
a bit in there. Shelves filled with smaller
items lined the walls while some of her
larger pieces of furniture were shoved into
the corners. Her trailer was parked in the
center. Going through all of this was going
to take a while.

She decided to start with the trailer. She
reached out to pull open the door. There was
a loud blast, and then nothing but darkness.

FOUR

Luke sat on a chair in the examining room at the hospital, looking at the scrapes and bandages on Melanie's face, feeling his gut twist into knots. After conducting numerous tests, the doctor had declared Melanie free of serious injury before heading to the nurse's station to complete the discharge process so Melanie could be released. Luke hated seeing those injuries on her face. And he was disappointed in himself for letting this happen. He should have told her not to go anywhere alone.

Her cousin, Anna, had also been allowed into the room. At the moment Anna stood to Luke's right, by a small sink and in front of a mirror. She was looking at her reflection and rearranging her short red hair while she chatted with Melanie.

Melanie shifted her gaze from her cousin until she was looking directly at Luke, and the knots in his stomach pulled tighter. Her hazel eyes were more green than brown, and despite what she'd been through, they still held a measure of trust when she looked at him. Trust that, right now, he wasn't sure he deserved.

She wore her brown hair long, with a straight line of bangs across her forehead. A small bandage above her left eyebrow pushed up her bangs, giving her a rumpled appearance that reminded him of how tired she must be.

The explosion had happened three hours ago, and he had no leads on who was responsible for it. The security cameras at the storage facility had been disabled. The device that had caused the explosion was not unique. And it was powerful enough to seriously damage the front of Melanie's truck.

Probably beyond repair. Luke had seen similar homemade devices while serving in the Middle East. Sadly, directions for how to make them were available on the internet, and the necessary supplies were easily obtained.

Luke didn't have much to go on other than the undeniable fact that someone was intent on killing Melanie. That made it imperative that he get every bit of information he could from her. He wasn't sure he had yet. Maybe she was holding something back.

He had to do his job. Press harder with more questions. Risk losing that glint of trust in her eyes when she looked at him. That's what they paid him for. To do what he had to do to get the results he needed.

"Anna, could you leave us alone for a minute, please?"

Melanie's cousin had been chattering about random, unimportant things as she fussed with her hair, obviously trying to lighten the mood. She stopped and turned to Luke and gave him a questioning look. Then she turned to Melanie.

"It's okay," Melanie said, her voice a little shaky. "I'll meet you out in the hallway in a couple of minutes." She glanced at Luke. "I'm sure this won't take long."

"Probably not," he agreed.

"All right." Anna grabbed her purse from a chair and walked out of the room.

The door was propped open. Luke got up, pushed aside the doorstop and then closed the door.

He went back to his chair, pulled it very close to the examining table, where Melanie was sitting, and then sat down. His knees were almost touching her shins. He'd carried out a few interrogations and he knew what he was watching for before he even started his questions.

The crazy idea crossed his mind that he wanted to reach out and smooth her bangs where they were caught up on that bandage above her eyebrow. He mercilessly killed that thought the second he realized what it was.

"What are you not telling me about these attacks on you and what might have triggered them?" he asked, and then he watched her face closely while waiting for her answer.

The trusting expression in her eyes became clouded with suspicion.

Luke was sorry to see that, but if he really wanted to help her—and he did—then pushing her buttons was a price he'd have to pay.

She stared at him for a moment, then stiffened her spine and leaned slightly back away from him. "I'm telling you everything I know," she said, her voice sounding high-pitched and indignant.

Maybe that was true. Maybe it wasn't.

"It's not my job to judge you," Luke said calmly. "But it is my job to protect you and that means I need all the information I can get. This is the third attempt on your life that I know of. Maybe there have been others.

There could be more attempts in the future, and right now I don't have any good leads on who the person behind this might be so I can stop them."

He paused and let that sink in. Her face turned even paler than it already was. He could see the fear in her eyes as they began to fill with unshed tears.

He felt like a jerk. But he was willing to do whatever it took to get the answers he needed. And he really wanted to stop this violence directed toward her right now. Before it was too late. Yes, he'd brought this up before. But it was difficult for him to believe she was randomly chosen as a target for these attacks. There had to be a reason.

"There isn't anything more for me to tell you," she said as she impatiently wiped away the tears now rolling down her cheeks. She turned from him, refusing to meet his gaze as she took a deep breath.

He waited until she finally turned her gaze back toward him again. This time she looked directly into his eyes, looking bold and defiant.

"If there's some piece of information you're holding back because you're embarrassed or you're afraid of getting in trouble or someone has threatened you, just tell me what it is. Keeping anything like that secret is not worth the risk of losing your life."

Luke was raised in a Christian household and he didn't for a moment think he was perfect. Far from it. In the military he'd gotten to know other soldiers who'd come from backgrounds very different from his own. Some of the situations they'd endured as children were just plain harrowing. Later, as a cop, he'd gotten a look into the secret lives that people tried to keep hidden from view. And he'd learned how hard some people worked to shake off a bad start in life or to simply hold themselves together while their life was falling apart.

So he did not care to judge people. Enforce the law, bring them to justice and hold them accountable? Yes. But judging them was not an activity he wanted to delve into.

In front of him, still sitting on the edge of the examining table, Melanie cleared her throat. "You're right," she said, sounding calmer and more composed. "It would be foolish of me to hide anything from you. And I'm not."

"Is it possible that someone sold you something valuable by mistake? Have you purchased a piece of furniture, an antique, anything that turned out to be worth more than the seller realized, and they wanted it back?"

"No, nothing like that has ever happened."

"Maybe someone accidentally left an item they valued in the drawer of a desk or dresser you bought. Maybe they hid something and now they're desperate to get it back."

"No one has ever said a word about anything like that to me."

She wasn't showing any of the usual signs

of someone lying or trying to hide the truth. His gut inclination was to believe her.

"All right," he said. "How about your memory? Is anything coming back to you?"

She tilted her head slightly and shifted her gaze to the left, squinting her eyes a little bit, as though she were trying hard to remember something. After a few seconds she shook her head and turned back to face him, her eyes darkened with unsettled emotion.

"What?" Luke asked. "What do you re-member?"

"I still can't remember anything. Not anything specific, anyway."

"What does that mean?" Luke fought to keep his tone neutral. At this point pushing her too hard might have the opposite effect of what he wanted. It might create stress that would continue to block her memories.

"At first, when I woke up in the woods outside the arena, and then saw you, it was like the prior two weeks had been completely erased from my memory. But now I have a feeling about what happened at the rodeo here in town before, well, before someone came after me and apparently took a shot at me and hit the tree branch that knocked me unconscious."

"Tell me about this feeling," Luke said. Maybe it would be helpful. Maybe it would just be a delusion formed in the brain of a woman who'd been violently attacked three times in seven days.

"I feel like I met somebody there. At the fairgrounds. What I mean is it felt like I met up with someone familiar."

"Who?"

"I don't know." Her shoulders slumped, making her look deflated.

"It happened here in Bowen, where you live, so you probably met with a lot of people you know that day. Friends or family coming by to check things out. Maybe you met with Anna." He made a mental note to talk to Anna so he could create a timeline of where she had been that day. He already knew that Melanie's cousin had been in the vicinity when Melanie had been attacked at the coffee shop. He didn't know where she'd been when the explosion had occurred at the storage facility this morning. But he would find out.

Right this moment he had no reason to suspect Anna of anything. But he had no concrete reason to clear her as a suspect, either. And his goal was to protect Melanie and catch the thug who'd come after her. Man or woman.

There was a quick knock on the door and then Anna pulled it open. An orderly stood beside her, with a wheelchair. "Whatever you two are discussing, I'm sure you can talk about it at home," she said, smiling at Melanie and then turning to Luke and raising her eyebrows, as if asking an unspoken question.

"We're finished." Luke got to his feet and then reached out to take hold of Melanie's upper arm and help her off the examining table.

He walked beside Melanie, Anna and the orderly as they headed down the hallway and eventually out the front door. Then he waited with Melanie while Anna went to fetch her car and drive it up to the hospital entrance.

"I'll follow you back to your house," Luke said.

"Thank you." Melanie nodded without looking at him. Her gaze seemed focused on the cluster of pine trees across the highway. A strong breeze had kicked up, lifting and buffeting around tendrils of hair on the top and sides of her head. For some reason that made her look more vulnerable to Luke, and his heart clenched a little.

"Do me a favor," he added. "Don't go anywhere alone."

"I won't."

Anna pulled up, Melanie got into her car and once again Luke followed her home.

He thought about her feeling that she'd met up with someone she knew at the fairgrounds. That was not the same thing as a memory, but it was the closest thing he had to a lead right now, so he would follow it and remember to ask about it each time he saw her. Maybe she would have clearer memories of what had happened at the fairgrounds later, given more time to heal.

The attacker might not only be someone known to her. It could be someone she was close to. Someone she trusted. Maybe, consciously or not, she didn't want to remember who it was. A choice that would leave her vulnerable to a next attack.

Standing in the sunroom at the back of Anna's house late the next morning, Melanie faced a stand of aspen trees. The gold leaves fluttering in the slight breeze gave Melanie a tranquil feeling that was quickly fading. That feeling of tranquility, though pleasant, could not be trusted. Somebody could be out there in the woods right now, watching and waiting for the perfect moment to take a shot at her.

She sighed and did her best to shake off that dark thought as she pried the lid off a can of varnish. The back wall and part of the ceiling on the extension to the old porch were made of a series of glass panels, and some of them could be opened. When she had a small project, she could work here and have decent ventilation.

After yesterday's explosion she felt like she'd earned the right to hide out in the house today, to not go to The Mercantile, to not go anywhere. But she couldn't just sit and stare out the window or at a TV screen, because that just made things worse. She'd tried reading right after Anna had left for work, but she kept forgetting what she'd just read. Her thoughts kept drifting to terrible images of what might have happened to her if she'd been a little farther inside her storage space when the device had exploded.

To keep herself occupied, she'd decided to do a little work, putting varnish on a small end table she'd rescued. Some people might think *rescued* was a silly word for an inanimate object, but Melanie didn't like to see salvageable things just tossed aside, especially old home furnishings with personality. So she'd learned to repair them. She'd taken her first jewelry-making class in high school, loved it and had made her own jewelry ever since. After the divorce, she knew she wanted to return home to Bowen, but there hadn't been a lot of job openings in town, so she'd taken the leap and started her own business.

She worked for a few minutes, applying varnish with a brush, and was already feeling soreness in her right shoulder, where she'd landed hard after the explosion, when her phone chimed. It was Luke, wanting to know if she'd be available to talk if he came by in a half hour. She texted him back, telling him that would be fine.

Actually it would be more than fine. In spite of the spats they'd had and her frustration when he'd asked her accusatory questions, she still felt better when he was around. Safer. Reassured. Even calmer, most of the time.

She also felt nervous and a little unsettled whenever she saw him. Like the protective barrier she'd built around herself after her marriage had ended was coming down, and to her surprise she was the one taking it down, brick by brick. Because she wanted to get to know Luke a little better. And he helped her feel strong enough to face her fears.

Along with her shoulder pain, she had a headache, so she headed toward the front of the house to get some over-the-counter pain relievers that were kept in the kitchen cabinet. Apparently she'd hit her head fairly hard, even though she'd landed on some boxes. Too bad she hadn't hit it hard enough to jar free some memories. How was it that she could remember all kinds of random things from her twenty-six years of life, but not those two weeks after she'd gone to sleep that night in the hotel in Wyoming?

And most important, why couldn't she remember the night of the attack here in Bowen? She was sure now that she'd met with someone she knew that night, but because she lived in Bowen, it could have been any of a number of people.

The doorbell rang. Luke had gotten here quickly. She went to answer the door, but just as she reached for the handle, a nudge of caution pressed her to first make certain it was him. She took a look through the window beside the door.

It wasn't Luke standing on the front porch. It was Peter. She'd often thought he looked younger than his age. Right now he looked especially young. And nervous. He glanced over his shoulder a couple of times and ran his apparently sweaty palms over his jean-clad thighs.

What would he be nervous about?

He'd been to the house several times, typically helping her move the larger pieces of furniture she was working on. She restored small items in the sunroom. For larger items, or any repair work that was going to be especially messy or potentially expose her to strong fumes, she worked in the detached garage alongside the house or in one of the storage sheds.

It wasn't especially unusual to see him here, but seeing him so obviously nervous made *her* feel uneasy. It was hard to believe he could intend her harm, but then she couldn't think of anyone she thought intended her harm. And yet someone obviously did.

She decided to ignore him and pretend no one was home. Unfortunately she made that decision a second too late. He saw her face through the narrow window and sharply nodded a greeting at her.

She sighed, feeling a flutter of anxiety in

the pit of her stomach. If he wanted to hurt her, he could break through a window easily enough. She might as well open the door and see what he wanted.

As she opened the door, she pulled her phone out of her back pocket and kept it in her hand, just in case.

"Good morning," she said, opening the door approximately half the width of her body. Whatever he had to say to her, he could say from the spot where he stood on the front porch.

Peter stared at her for a moment, then shook his head sadly. "I sure am sorry to see more bruises on you, Ms. Graham."

She'd had a few new red marks on her face after the explosion yesterday. By this morning they'd darkened into purple bruises on her cheek and jaw.

"Is there something I can do for you?" Melanie asked him.

"I just wanted to talk to you."

"Okay. What you like to talk to me about?"

She still hadn't made a move to let him into the house.

"You can't really believe I'd do anything to hurt you," he said, with his eyes wide and his expression sorrowful.

She just looked at him without answering. Until a week ago she didn't think anyone would intentionally harm her. Now she had to be careful around nearly everyone.

"Okay," he said. "I'm here because, when I showed up to work at The Mercantile a few minutes ago, Diana said Lieutenant Baxter had just been there, looking for me." He fumbled in his pocket, pulled out a business card and held it up to show her. She couldn't read the print from this far away, but she recognized the embossed gold star of the county sheriff's department. It looked like the card Luke had given her.

"I just wanted to talk to you first, before I talk to the cops," he said, his voice shaking. "I wanted to know if you suspect me of trying to kill you."

"I don't know what to say," she said. "I don't specifically suspect anyone. And yet I have to be suspicious of everyone." The truth of that hit her hard as she said the words. "Lieutenant Baxter should be here any minute," she added. "Why don't you wait and talk to him?"

Peter's eyes grew wide and he glanced nervously over his shoulder. He took a couple of steps back, but then she could see him take a deep breath and relax his shoulders, as though he were collecting his emotions.

He gestured behind himself, at the steps on the front porch. "I'll just sit out here and wait for him."

Melanie felt a tug at her heart. She'd never owned her own business before. Never had an employee. But when she'd needed to hire an assistant, Diana had recommended Peter and he'd been a good choice. Helpful and polite. She couldn't make him sit out here, on the front steps. That just felt wrong.

"It's okay—you go on back inside the

house," he said, as though recognizing her dilemma. "I understand. You need to be careful. I'm fine out here."

She was just about to close the door and text Luke to ask how much longer he'd be when she spotted his sheriff's department pickup truck pulling up to the curb in front of the house.

Luke got out and headed briskly toward the house. He wore dark sunglasses, so Melanie couldn't see his eyes, but his gaze seemed fixed toward the front of the house, where she stood.

"What are you doing here?" Luke called out to Peter, his voice tight with tension as he approached the steps. He didn't wait for an answer as he continued forward and up the steps, positioning himself between Peter and Melanie, who still had the door held open. Finally he glanced toward Melanie and gave her a quick nod, which she supposed was meant to be a greeting.

"I'm here to talk to Ms. Graham," Peter said in answer to Luke's question.

"About what?"

"Peter knows you want to talk to him, so he waited here," Melanie said. Her feelings were torn between fear that Luke had some substantial reason for his obvious suspicion of the young man and a sense of responsibility toward her employee that compelled her to look out for him.

"Well, that's an interesting coincidence," Luke said. "Because I came here to talk to you about Peter."

On the other side of the street, Sheila, one of the neighbors, seemed to be taking an inordinate amount of time unloading a single bag of groceries from her car. And she kept glancing toward Melanie's house. "Why don't the both of you come inside," Melanie said. Now that Luke was here, she felt safer. She opened the door wider and took a step back into the house to make room for them to come in.

In the front room Luke gestured for Peter to sit, while he remained standing. Good manners compelled Melanie to offer them something to drink. Both men declined.

"Did Peter tell you he comes from a criminal family?" Luke asked.

Melanie laughed. She couldn't help it. Some of it was probably due to nervous tension. But, also, the idea was ridiculous.

Except Peter wasn't laughing. Instead he looked even paler. Almost like he was getting sick. He clasped his hands tightly in his lap.

"Peter?" She started to move toward him, and Luke took a step sideways, keeping himself between her and Peter. Which was silly. Peter was no threat. Was he?

Peter turned away from her at first. And then, after a moment, he turned back to her. This time his face was flushed in anger, and his brows were drawn together in a scowl. "I'm not like them!"

Stunned, Melanie turned to Luke for an explanation.

"I was running background checks on people who I know are connected to you, looking to see who might be suspect. Turns out Peter Altman was Peter Cameron until shortly after he turned eighteen, when he had his name changed. If he had told me that fact at the beginning of this investigation, it certainly would have gotten my attention. And it's something I thought you should know. If you didn't already."

"What are you talking about?" Melanie asked, stunned and trying to follow what Luke was telling her.

"There are several members of the Cameron family who have decided to live life as career criminals. Not organized crime. Just theft. All kinds of theft. Strong-arm robbery. Residential burglaries. Commercial burglaries. Car theft. Theft from *storage spaces*. You name it."

"Does Diana know?" Melanie asked Peter.

"No!" Peter snapped. And then he shook his head. "When I was old enough to realize I didn't want to be like my dad, didn't want to be like my older half brothers, I moved out of the house and in with my grandfather. My mom's dad. My mom died a long time ago."

"And you went to work creating a cover story so you could stay above suspicion while you continued in the family business," Luke stated.

"No!"

"When I was checking out your background and running your name—or *names*, after I found out about the second identity—I came across the oddest bit of information. During the time frame of that rodeo in Leopold, when Melanie was there, your brothers, Sam and Rick, were also there. They were riding together in a van and they got pulled over for speeding. I can't help wondering if there's a connection between your brothers and Melanie being in that town at the same time and what happened to her later."

"What kind of connection?" Melanie asked, starting to feel shaky. Her world as she understood it kept changing and she was getting tired of it.

Luke shrugged. He was still watching Peter closely, as though he thought he might pull out a weapon at any moment. "There's that big flea market in Leopold, when the rodeo is in town. A lot of stolen items get sold there. Sometimes drugs are sold there, too. It's a place where criminals can meet up and make their arrangements in plain sight. And it's a good opportunity for people on parole or probation to *accidentally* meet up with former illegal-business partners that they are not supposed to have anything to do with."

"But how is that connected to me?" Melanie said.

"You said you walked around the flea market, looking for things to resell. Maybe you saw Peter's brothers trying to sell stolen goods. Or maybe you overheard them say something that could get them into trouble."

"But I wouldn't have recognized them if I saw them. I wouldn't have paid any attention to what they were saying. I didn't even know Peter had brothers."

"They might not realize that you don't know who they are. Because I'm sure they know who *you* are."

A chill passed over the surface of her skin. "Why would you say that?"

Luke gestured toward Peter, who had turned toward them and was listening closely.

"Peter is working with you. He's working with other people at The Mercantile, where he's in a position of trust. I'm sure his brothers have been in there to see who he is working with, to see what opportunities might exist."

"To steal things?" she asked.

"Or to get Peter to steal things. Or to get

him to give them the alarm code to the security system there. Or maybe let them know when there's an unusually large amount of cash or valuables on hand at The Mercantile."

Peter shook his head. "I would never do that."

"Maybe you wouldn't want to, but as soon as you started keeping the family connection a secret, you set yourself up for blackmail."

Peter, who'd been sitting very rigidly, slumped back against the sofa cushion. Then he tilted his head back and stared up at the ceiling for a moment. "Why are you talking to me? Why not my brothers?"

"I wanted to talk to you immediately because you spend time around Melanie and my top priority is keeping her safe."

"And you thought I might be a danger to her?"

"Yes."

"Do you still think that?"

Luke paused before he answered. "Let's just say you're still a person of interest to me."

Peter slowly got to his feet. He turned to Melanie. "Thank you for giving me the opportunity to work for you. I've really enjoyed it."

"Wait," Melanie said, holding up a staying hand. "Let's just slow things down a bit. I didn't say you were fired." She wasn't a woman to take unnecessary risks. And she'd watched enough true-crime TV to be wary. But she also knew that what other people thought sometimes wasn't true. And despite the old adage people liked to repeat, sometimes the apple *did* fall far from the tree. She had experience with that. She'd been determined to *not* be like her parents. Her father had walked out on them when she was very young. Her mother, anxious to find a new husband, had convinced herself that a woman's value lay mainly in her appearance.

"I think you need to make sure Diana knows the truth about you and your family," Melanie said to Peter. "And see if she's still willing to keep you employed at The Mercantile. Make sure everybody else there knows, because they're going to find out the truth, anyway. And if everybody knows, your brothers can't blackmail you."

"All right."

"I did send a couple of deputies to talk to your brothers while I came here," Luke said. He glanced at Melanie. "According to their driver's license information, both brothers live at the same address."

Peter nodded and got to his feet. "First thing I'm going to do is go home and talk to my grandpa. And then I'll call Diana." He exchanged goodbyes with Melanie, while Luke kept a close eye on him, and then he left. Luke locked the door behind him.

"Will your deputies search Peter's brothers' home for residue from making the explosive used at the storage place?" Melanie asked.

"Only if the brothers allow it. We don't

have enough evidence of probable cause to get a search warrant. Not yet." His phone chimed. He pulled it out of the holder on his belt and glanced at the screen. "It's one of the deputies I sent to talk to Peter's brothers. I need to get back to the office."

Melanie walked him to the door. Before he opened it, he turned to her. "I realize if you live in a world of people who are decent and trustworthy, it's hard to believe how evil some people can be. Even people you think you know. *Please* be careful. I don't want to come looking for you and find out I've arrived too late. I need you to stay safe long enough for me to untangle this web you're caught up in."

Melanie crossed her arms over her chest, unsettled by what she'd just learned about Peter and trying to hold herself together. "I'm doing my best."

FIVE

"Are you supposed to have that?" Luke shoved a pitchfork into a bale of hay and looked directly at the black-and-brown dog standing in front of him with a sock in its mouth.

In response Billy Clyde gave his tail a few uncertain wags before lowering his head and averting his gaze. He did not, however, drop the sock.

The standoff was taking place in the stables on the Baxter family ranch. It was Sunday morning, early enough that it was still dark outside, and Luke was taking care of the animals. It was one of the main things on the ranch that had to be done every single day.

Oftentimes Luke was scheduled to report to work on Sundays. When he wasn't, like today, he took care of a few chores so Jake could sleep in and then have a leisurely breakfast with Kayla and Alan before getting them dressed for Sunday school and taking them to the little country church near the ranch.

If Luke wasn't scheduled to work on a Sunday, he went to church with them. Except for the times when his work week had shown him too much of the dark side of human nature, or he found his thoughts mired in some of his worst memories of his experiences in combat. On those occasions he stayed home, alone, figuring he'd be rotten company, anyway. He realized that those times when he felt out of sorts were probably the times when he really should push himself to go to church. It was a challenge he was working on.

Whether or not he was going to church today was still up in the air. He'd been thinking about Melanie Graham this morning. About the repeated attacks on her, and the grim reality that someone with evil intentions toward her was in his town and he needed to do something about it. Terrible things happened to good people fairly often. He'd witnessed it. And that thought had put him in a dark mood.

He shifted his thoughts back to Billy Clyde, who was still in front of him.

Since the sock in the dog's mouth was too big to belong to either of the kids, and it didn't look like anything Luke owned, that meant it probably belonged to Jake. And in the spirit of brotherly love, Luke decided his brother could look after his own socks.

"Come here, buddy," he said to Billy Clyde, while crouching down and extending a hand toward him.

The dog dipped his head a little bit lower, as though he thought he were in trouble. Great, he'd scared Billy Clyde. Luke sometimes got that edgy reaction from people, even when he wasn't wearing his sheriff's department uniform. He was a big guy and his voice was deep.

Right now he just wanted to pet the dog, but the animal was afraid of him.

He moved forward a little and reached out again to Billy Clyde. The mutt turned his muzzle away, then rolled his eyes toward Luke, giving him the old side-eye. In an instant his tail started wagging furiously and he turned and sprinted out the barn door, victorious, with the stolen sock still clenched in his teeth.

"Seriously, dog?" Luke called out to the empty air. "I wasn't going to try to take your sock!" In the quiet of the barn, Luke could hear himself laughing. Maybe the day wasn't going to take the dark turn he'd been afraid of, after all.

He went back to work, making sure the animals were taken care of. About the time he'd finished, after the sun was up and the sky had lightened to the shade of faded denim, his phone chimed with a text message. He hoped it was his brother, saying that Luke had a plate of warm chocolate chip pancakes waiting for him on the dining room table. Instead he was surprised to see that it was a text from Melanie Graham.

Going to nine o'clock services, church near our house.

He stood, looking at his phone's screen for a moment, trying to figure out why she'd sent him the message. He had not asked her to inform him every time she left the house. Only that she not go anywhere alone.

Was she nervous about going? Was there a specific reason she was nervous, beyond the obvious and understandable fear that she might be attacked again?

He knew her well enough by now to figure she wasn't asking for his permission or approval.

Maybe she wanted Luke to wait outside and keep an eye on things during the service.

He could text her back or call her and try to clarify things, but he was afraid she would feel put on the spot and discount her concerns.

It might be a good idea for him to go into town and check on her. Officially today was his day off, but the sheriff's department had a relatively small number of patrol officers for the sparsely populated yet geographically large county, and occasionally that meant deputies needed to put in a few extra hours on their scheduled day off.

He'd made the decision almost without realizing it. He was already walking up the rise toward the house, texting his captain, letting him know what he was planning to do.

Luke didn't have much time if he wanted to get to town before the service started. Inside the house he was greeted by the sizzle and smell of bacon frying. He headed into the kitchen, where he greeted his brother, who was busy at the stove. He grabbed a few strips of the cooked bacon, and then told Jake he was heading into town. Chewing on the bacon, he hustled up the stairs to hurriedly get showered and dressed.

As he walked down the long upstairs hallway, he passed his nephew's bedroom. The door was open and Luke glanced in. "Good morning," he called out to Alan, who was sitting up in bed, with his hair tousled, looking half asleep.

The boy mumbled something indecipherable in return, while staring into space.

Billy Clyde, who was lying on his side, at the foot of the bed, lazily thumped his tail a couple of times. The sock that wily animal had earlier was nowhere in sight.

Luke pulled his truck to the curb across the street from the little white clapboard church, just a few blocks from Anna's house, and glanced at the top of the steeple, where the bell was still ringing. A few last-minute arrivals—all of them with children in tow, he noted—headed up the steps and went inside.

His cop mindset was running in high gear as he looked up and down the street, scanning for anything out of the ordinary. From what he could tell, he was the only person waiting out here in a vehicle. But he could only see this side of the church. He couldn't see what was happening on the other side of the building. Or inside of it.

It had only been two days since the explosion at the storage place. That was the third attack on Melanie. That he knew of. Whoever wanted her dead was likely frustrated that she was still alive, and possibly at a point where he'd do anything to finish the deed.

It was chilling to think that an assailant would attempt to attack someone in a church. But foolish to assume they wouldn't.

He straightened his tie as he got out of

his truck, then reached back in for his suit coat and slipped it on. Lots of churches in the area were filled with people dressed casually on Sunday mornings, but Luke was carrying a gun in a shoulder holster and he wanted to keep it hidden. Both because he didn't want to make churchgoers nervous and because he didn't want any potential bad guy to know he was being watched by a cop.

Or potential bad *guys* to know. Maybe there was more than one involved. Like maybe Peter Altman's two career-thief brothers.

Luke started across the street, scanning his surroundings and frustrated by the vagueness of the case. With three brazen attempts on Melanie's life, you'd think there would be more concrete evidence.

The fact that she couldn't remember that two-week block of time, up to and including being chased and shot at outside the fairgrounds, made it more challenging. And frightening. There was no telling whom she might trust in her day-to-day life that would attempt to kill her the next time he got a chance. And the next time he might be successful.

As Luke walked around the church, he could hear the congregation inside singing. Everything outside the building looked normal. No one was lurking in the vicinity, although after he finished walking the perimeter, a back door opened. A man stepped out onto the stoop, followed by a girl who was maybe five-years-old. She was red-faced, sucking in her bottom lip, clearly in trouble. The man squatted down so he was at eye level with her and began talking in a calm voice.

Through the open door Luke could hear the pastor concluding a prayer and then beginning his sermon. It would be good to go inside, take a seat in the back and keep an eye on things. Just in case. And it would probably be good to attend a service, even though he'd woken up in a dark mood this morning. A mood made a little darker by the reality that he was about to attend a church service to make sure a worshipper stayed safe. Sometimes it seemed like the world got more unpredictable every day.

He entered the sanctuary and stood against the back wall. The pastor saw him and gave him a slight nod. They had crossed paths professionally a few times. Mainly at the emergency room at the hospital. Luke glanced around and didn't see anything out of the ordinary. He did, however, recognize Melanie. Even though she sat up near the front, he knew her by her hair and the slight tilt to her head. He'd noticed before that she tilted her head when she was listening closely to someone. Anna was seated beside her.

Luke sat down in a pew, in the last row. He listened to the sermon. He prayed. And he regularly shifted his attention toward the doors, just in case someone dangerous was lurking there. When the service ended, his spirit felt lighter and he was glad he came.

Melanie's eyes widened in surprise and then a smile flashed across her face when she saw him. Seeing her bruises made his gut tighten, even though he'd already known they were there.

"I didn't mean for you to come here when I texted you," she said, a blush of red coloring her cheeks. "I guess… Well, I don't know what I thought when I texted you."

People squeezing past them on their way down the aisle pushed them a little closer together and Luke noticed she smelled flowery, like lavender. And looking down at her, he could see that her brown hair had a few streaks of copper running through it. And maybe some gold.

What was he doing? Why was he studying her *hair*?

"Someone is trying to hurt you and you're scared," he said. He forced himself to look away from her for a moment and spotted Anna talking to a couple of other women and a man. Then he turned back to Melanie. "If I were in your place, I'd be texting somebody to watch my back when I left the house, too."

She nodded while twisting both hands around the handle of her purse. "Thank you."

They made their way toward Anna and her friends, who were making plans to go out to eat, and they invited Melanie and Luke to join them.

"I think I'll just go back to the house," Melanie said. "I don't believe I'd feel comfortable sitting in a restaurant."

Looking stricken, Anna quickly apologized to her cousin. "I wasn't thinking," she said. She was starting to back out of the group's lunch plans when Luke offered to take Melanie to grab some coffee and pastries that they could take back to the house. Luke would stay with her until Anna came home.

"If that's all right with you," he said to Melanie.

She looked about as surprised as he felt.

He'd pretty much made the offer before he realized what he was doing. But then he told himself he was doing his job. Protecting a citizen. He wasn't a social kind of guy. It would just be coffee and a huckleberry scone. It was nothing.

Except that he *did* feel a slight pull of tension while he waited for her response. And then a little more tension when she agreed.

After leaving the church and getting their coffees and scones, as well as some maple bars and apple fritters, Luke asked if she'd be willing to make a change in their plans. "How do you feel about going by the sheriff's department, and I'll show you some mug shots of Peter's brothers, plus a few of their unsavory friends?" The deputies Luke had sent to talk to Peter's brothers weren't able to make contact with them, but they would keep trying. Meanwhile, if Melanie looked at the pictures, she might recognize someone. "Maybe seeing them will jog your memory of those missing couple of weeks and what happened to you at the fairgrounds, here in town."

She didn't answer right away and when he glanced over, she was shaking her head sadly. "Sure, we can do that," she said. "But I hate to think Peter could be mixed up in all of this."

"Career criminals are usually good manipulators. It's also possible that someone in his family is involved, but that Peter isn't."

"People can be different from the other members of their family," she said after a moment. "I'm different from my parents."

"How so?"

"My dad took off when I was little. Just left me and my mother with hardly any warning. I would never do that to anyone. Before he left he said some mean things to my mom that made her believe her appearance was the reason their marriage failed. She lost weight, focused a lot on her looks and worked hard to convince me that looking pretty was the most important thing in a woman's life. Well, that and finding a husband as quickly as you could before you lost your looks."

Luke had no idea how to comment on any of that. It sounded ridiculous to him.

"I took her advice, even though in my heart I felt like what she was telling me was wrong. At eighteen I married a guy I barely knew. We never discussed the important things we should have talked about. And he had secrets. When he filed for divorce, I found out he had a whole other life I didn't know about. A girlfriend he'd kept hidden. Friends he'd met through her who'd never even heard of me. Secret credit card debt he'd racked up while trying to impress those same friends. And a growing dependence on alcohol to help deaden his conscience."

She was quiet for a moment. "I had good friends in California. People I met at church. Ben never wanted to spend any time around them." She took a deep breath. "Anyway, I love my mom, but she's still focused on appearances. And she only wants to have frivolous, surface-level conversations all the time. Not anything substantial."

Luke wasn't so crazy about deep, rambling conversations himself. The point of life was to deal with things, not talk them to death. That was his father's motto while raising both of his boys, and it had seemed to work pretty well. Although, actually, Jake had become more of a talker over time. Janelle might have had something to do with that.

"My dad lived in this county from the time he was about three years old," Luke said. "I left soon after high school, traveled the world and the only reason I'm here now is to help out Jake. When his kids are a little bigger, I'll take off again." So, yeah, he was different from his family, too.

And apparently he was the only one in the family who got addicted to the rush of adrenaline that being in the military had given him. Oddly enough that rush helped to quiet something in him. It was a compulsion he'd developed soon after his mom had died. Doing things that were dangerous. Taking risks. It helped shove aside the sadness and the loneliness. He got that adrenaline rush, once in a while, working as a sheriff's deputy these days, but not often enough. Crime in Miles County was usually pretty run-of-the-mill.

Melanie didn't say anything else until they got to the sheriff's department offices. And that tension he'd felt earlier, when he'd invited her to get coffee and pastries with him, had vanished. Which was good. He recognized that tension for what it was—maybe a little bit of interest between them—but he wasn't looking to date. And he definitely wasn't in the market for a wife.

Inside the sheriff department's office, they sat down at Luke's desk and dove into the pastries while he brought up the booking photos he wanted her to take a look at. Peter's oldest half brother, Sam, was heavyset, with hard, flat eyes, and a sneer on his lips.

His other half brother, Rick, had a slender build like Peter and stared into the camera, with his jaw slightly dropped as though he weren't sure what was going on.

Melanie looked at both pictures for a while. "They look a little familiar," she finally said.

Luke's heartbeat sped up. A lead. Finally they had a lead.

"But I don't know if they look familiar because I've seen them somewhere," Melanie said. "Or if it's because they both look a little like Peter."

Trying not to show his disappointment, Luke asked her a few questions about where she might have seen them or if they reminded her of anything. Unfortunately she had no useful answers for him. He showed her pictures of their known criminal associates, but they didn't look familiar to her, either.

When he brought her back to the house, Anna was already there. Melanie had texted her earlier about the change in plans, letting her know she and Luke were going by the sheriff's department, so she wouldn't worry.

Luke walked Melanie inside the house and stayed for a few minutes, reminding the two women to keep all the doors and windows locked before finally asking for and receiving permission to just go ahead and check them all himself. Before he left he again talked to Anna about getting an alarm system installed. "I know you want to believe you're both completely safe in your own home," he said to her. "But you're not. For all we know the person intent on *killing* Melanie has already been in this house. Either as an invited guest or as a stranger who broke into your house and you never knew it."

The wide-eyed expression of fear that immediately appeared on Anna's face told him he'd hit his mark. He certainly didn't enjoy making her feel afraid, but right now keeping her emotions on edge just might save her cousin's life, as well as her own, since she could be caught in the cross fire if there was another attack.

An alarm system didn't guarantee anyone's safety, but it would give them a heads-up if anyone was inside their house or on the property immediately around it. And that would give them the chance to escape, call for help or both.

By the time their conversation ended, Anna was already looking up alarm-system companies on her phone.

When Luke got back into the cab of his truck, it felt especially empty without Melanie alongside him. Which was odd, because he normally preferred riding alone.

As soon as he realized the direction his thoughts were going in, he forced himself to redirect them. He wasn't looking for a romantic attachment; he was searching for a dangerous criminal who was intent on killing Melanie. And he still had no idea who that assailant was.

He sat in the truck for a moment and looked at Anna's house. The Bowen city cops would be patrolling the neighborhood regularly and even parking outside the house when they could, to keep an eye on things. It was probably the best Luke could ask for right now, but it didn't feel like enough. What he wanted to do was stay there himself. Personally keep her safe. Because the thought of anything happening to her twisted his gut into knots.

But right now that was not the best thing for her. The bad guy would likely not give up and move on while Luke stayed hunkered down at the house with Melanie, protecting her. If the attacker couldn't get to Melanie, he might just lie low until everyone thought the threat had passed. Then he would launch an attack on her in the future, when she was no longer being protected, and that would likely prove fatal.

Somebody had to go out and hunt down the mysterious attacker, and Luke wanted to be the man to do it. He fired up the truck's engine and headed back to his office, intent on looking over case notes, making some phone calls, getting some kind of lead on the attacker and capturing him before it was too late.

Every time Melanie had been to Wyoming, it had been windy, and today was no different. She usually didn't mind it, but right now the wind had an unsettling feel to it. Normally she brought someone with her on these remote-location sales trips, but this time she hadn't. Going to the rodeo to sell her jewelry and furniture in Leopold had been a last-minute decision.

In an instant, late-morning turned to dusk. Melanie was out of Wyoming now, passing through Montana and almost to Idaho, determined to get her truck and trailer back home without stopping. Sales of her signature jewelry, plus the antiques and small pieces of repurposed furniture, had gone well. Lots of artists and crafters in the region traveled to the same venues to sell their wares, and Melanie had bumped into several people she knew. Although no one specific came to mind.

And then she was standing outside her truck, and it was getting dark. In the strange way of dreams, she knew this was an entirely different day. That time had passed. She was in a parking lot. There were people near the entrance to the fairgrounds in Bowen, but no one nearby.

Except there was someone nearby. Someone who shoved what felt like the muzzle of a gun into the back of her neck, slapped a gloved hand over her mouth and hissed, "Let's go."

Terror ripped through the midsection of Melanie's body, and when she opened her eyes she was already sitting up, her stomach churning and her heart thundering in her chest.

There was a split second when she didn't

know where she was. And then, in the faint light of early morning, she recognized the bentwood rocker with the needlepoint cushion she'd made, and she realized she was safe at home, in her bedroom, at Anna's house.

And Anna was speaking to someone. Loudly. She was probably on the phone with her husband, who'd been deployed overseas.

At the moment Melanie had no interest in what her cousin was saying. She wanted to concentrate on that weird series of dreams she'd just had, and she was afraid if she shifted her attention to anything else, her memory of those dreams would vanish.

Her memory. Was that what those dreams were? Memories? And did that mean the part where she'd dreamed about the man shoving the gun into the back of her neck was real?

A wave of fear washed over her, nearly as strong as that gut-punch of terror that had woken her, and she started to tremble. Her skin was clammy. And she could feel tendrils of hair sticking to the sweat at her temples.

Sometimes people start to remember things they've forgotten when they're ready and can handle it, the doctor had told her. Melanie wasn't ready. She couldn't handle it. And yet it was almost like the dream was carrying over into wakefulness. Images were forming in her mind, though the context and order of things was vague.

She said a quick prayer, asking for strength and courage, and then threw off the covers and got out of bed. She needed to text Luke and let him know she was starting to remember things. But even before that, she needed to grab her notebook and jot down what she was remembering before she could forget it again.

Having a chunk of time in her life that she couldn't remember was a horrible experience. Remembering someone shoving a gun against her neck and covering her mouth so she couldn't scream for help didn't feel much better. But at least by remembering the event, there was the chance she could identify the person who had pulled the gun on her. Presumably the person who was behind *all* of the attacks on her. And hopefully she could get him locked up so he couldn't harm her or anyone else ever again.

She quickly made a list of what she could remember. There were lots of gaps in time and some of it didn't make sense. But it was what she had.

She slipped on her robe and went to tell Anna that her memory was coming back. When she pulled open the door, she was startled to see Anna standing in the hallway, right outside.

"Sorry, I didn't mean to scare you," Anna quickly muttered. "I was just wondering if you were okay. I was on the phone with Tyler and thought I heard you make a noise up here, like a yelp or something. I wanted to check if you were all right, but I didn't want to wake you."

Had Melanie screamed when she had awoken from the nightmare? Maybe that was the sound Anna had heard.

"I'm starting to remember things," Melanie said.

Anna's eyes grew wide. "Like what?"

Melanie described some of the different fragments of events she now remembered, as she led the way downstairs and into the kitchen, where she grabbed a mug from a hook under the counter and then poured herself some coffee.

It didn't take long to describe everything to Anna. "Now I need to let Lieutenant Baxter know that I've gotten some memories back," she said, pulling her phone out of her robe pocket to text him.

"*Lieutenant* Baxter?" Anna said in a teasing tone as she raised an eyebrow. "Don't you mean *Luke*?"

Melanie ignored her and sent the text. A couple of minutes later, her phone rang.

"Is that the lieutenant?" Anna asked in a

singsong voice before flashing Melanie a wide grin.

It was him.

Cheeks burning, Melanie turned away and walked out into the living room.

"Do you remember who shot at you at the fairgrounds?" Luke asked as soon as she answered.

If only she did and everything could be wrapped up so easily. "No." She took a deep breath and told him what she did remember about being held at gunpoint, feeling a little taken aback to find herself trembling in fear again. The event had taken place eight days ago, but recovering the memory of it now made it feel like it had just happened.

"Are you at the house?" Luke asked.

"Yes."

"I'll be there in twenty minutes."

Melanie disconnected and looked down at her bathrobe. She needed to take a shower and get dressed. "Luke will be here in twenty minutes," she called over her shoulder, to Anna, as she headed back upstairs. She didn't linger long enough to hear any comments her cousin might want to share.

She was out of the shower and already dressed in jeans and a long-sleeve T-shirt when she heard a knock at the front door, followed by the sound of Luke and Anna talking. She glanced at the clock on her nightstand. He was right on time.

She hesitated for a moment, trying to decide if she should dry her hair and put on some makeup before going downstairs. But this was not a social call. He was a cop doing his job and she shouldn't waste his time. And why should she care how she looked?

If she were honest, Anna's joke about the *lieutenant* did get under Melanie's skin just a bit. Because there were moments when she felt a little spark of connection with Luke.

But she needed to keep her attention focused on staying alive. And keeping her business afloat, because she had no one else to rely on financially. He'd told her that he meant to leave town when his brother and the children were emotionally back on their feet. Probably within a year. And that he was a cop, and before that a soldier, because he was an adrenaline junkie.

Protecting her while someone was trying to kill her was apparently enough to keep his interest now, but her case wouldn't remain unsolved forever. At least she hoped not. Which meant their relationship was like a house built on sand.

Her relationship with her ex-husband had definitely been built on sand. It had just taken her a while to realize it. And then she'd fooled herself into believing she could change him. She wasn't going down that road again.

When she walked down the stairs and saw Luke, her breath caught in her throat. She swallowed hard, shook off the feeling and walked over to greet him. They sat in the living room and it didn't take long to tell him everything she remembered. He took detailed notes.

"Let me know when you remember anything else," he said when she walked him to the door a half hour later, after Anna had plied them with oatmeal muffins and coffee, and then vanished from the living room.

She nodded. "I will."

As soon as she realized she was still standing there, staring at him as he walked back to his sheriff's department pickup truck, she made herself shut the door and walk away.

There was nothing between them. There never would be. He would be moving on. She had a life to rebuild once the psychopath who was trying to kill her was caught. There was no chance that anything lasting could develop between them.

SIX

Luke sat in the waiting room of Melanie's doctor's office. He couldn't help thinking back to when he was a kid and his mom was sick. He'd spent a fair amount of time back then, sitting beside his dad and his little brother, peppering his dad with questions about what was happening to his mom and what was going to happen to *him*.

He was young and self-centered then, as kids tend to be. Fearful, worried and unable to understand at the time that, when his dad had told him to sit quietly and stop jabbering about every thought that crossed his mind, it was likely because his dad was at the end of his rope emotionally. And later, after Mom was gone, it was probably easier for his dad if everybody just kept a lid on their thoughts and feelings as much as possible.

They had all pretty much done that, too. Until Jake had met Janelle and she got him to open up. And of course remembering that now had Luke thinking about Janelle. Like his mom, she'd also been dealt what felt like an unfairly short lifespan. But she'd touched a lot of lives in a very positive way, and she'd left behind two beautiful children to keep Jake company. Painful as the situation was, there were still things to be grateful for.

The door from the back area of the doctor's office to the waiting room opened and Melanie stepped through. When Luke had called her this morning to check up on her, she'd told him she had this appointment. Her doctor had insisted on closely spaced follow-up visits after the explosion at the storage space. She was concerned about possible cumulative damage after the three attacks on Melanie's life.

Luke had offered to take her to the appointment. He wanted her to be safe and he had a couple of things to talk about with her, anyway.

At this morning's briefing with the sheriff, Luke had reported that Melanie's memory was starting to come back, though what she'd remembered so far wasn't too helpful. He'd also suggested that he take her back out to the fairgrounds, where the shooting had happened, and ask her again to tell him what she'd remembered of that evening, from start to finish. Maybe she'd remember something new.

"We don't have enough deputies for you to focus exclusively on Melanie Graham's case," the sheriff had told Luke before ending their meeting. "But I will shift some of your assignments to give you more time to work on it."

Luke had a couple of hours today to question Melanie and hopefully prompt more of her lost memories to resurface. Now that her appointment was over, he wanted to ask what the doctor had to say. But as a lawman, here on professional business, that might not be an appropriate question, given patient privacy laws. So he settled for, "How are you feeling?" as they walked across the waiting room and out into the hallway of the medical building.

She smiled at him, and his gaze lingered on her face a little longer than it probably should have. But he liked looking at her. "I'm fine," she said. "The doctor told me I should be prepared to remember more things from that period of time when my memories had vanished."

Luke nodded. "Good. Would you be willing to go back to the fairgrounds and walk around? See if you can remember anything new?"

"All right."

"It's getting close to noon. We should probably grab some food and take it with us to the fairgrounds and it eat there." He needed to make good use of the time he had with her today. If they ate in a restaurant, he couldn't talk with her about the investigation, because people could be eavesdropping. "What kind of food sounds good?" he asked.

"Italian," she said without hesitation. "I can always eat Italian."

Gennaro's had the best Italian food in town, and while there wasn't an app you could use to order, they did have a take-out menu posted online. Luke called in their order and had Melanie go with him inside the restaurant to pick it up. So far she'd only been attacked when she was alone. So the obvious solution was to never leave her alone.

They drove to the Bowen Fairgrounds with their food. Luke had already exchanged texts with Don Chastain to make certain there were no events going on today. Don was not only head of event security, but also site manager. He'd assured Luke that Melanie would be able to walk around the grounds without being bothered by employ-ees or customers.

"You sure you're okay with this?" Luke asked as they waited outside the main build-ing for Don to unlock the door and let them in. He didn't want to push her to do anything that might be emotionally traumatizing. For one thing she'd been through a lot in a short amount of time, and there was only so much a person could take. He knew that from his own experiences in combat. And on a prac-tical level, being upset might close down the flow of memories that had just started. And without the memory of who had attacked her, she was in grave danger.

Don showed up to open the door and waved them in.

"I can walk around here and see what I remember," Melanie said, grabbing the bag from Gennaro's, which was loaded with a large container of fettucine Alfredo and a big six-cheese calzone. "This psychopath who's trying to kill me is already taking away my life by forcing me to hide much of the time, and I'm tired of it. I want to catch him."

It seemed to Luke like the beginning of the recovery of her memory had also brought with it a change in Melanie's attitude. Which could be a blessing. Confidence was good. So was determination. But if that led to her taking risks with her safety, or becoming impatient with the investigation and trying to solve things on her own, it would be a problem. A very big one.

Inside the building, Don led them to an office where they could have some privacy. Luke invited him to join them for lunch, assuring him that they'd intentionally bought enough food for him to have some, but he declined, telling them he had to be on a conference call in a few minutes.

Melanie wanted to sit next to the window with a view of the forested area outside, but Luke told her it was a bad idea and pulled a couple of chairs over to a table at the opposite end of the room. Then he flicked off the overhead light. "Plenty of natural light in here," he said, gesturing toward the window. "And we don't want to make you an easy target."

She was taking the food and plastic cutlery out of the bag, and when he made his comment she hesitated for a few seconds. Then she resumed what she was doing without comment.

Luke felt like a jerk. She'd been a little happy and feeling more certain of things, because her memory was coming back. But it was his job to protect her and remind her that she needed to stay cautious.

"Seems a little odd to be worried about a window if we're going to be outside in a few minutes," she finally said.

Good point. "We have to take *some* risks," Luke said. "There's no avoiding it. Walking around the property to see if you remember anything significant is a worthwhile risk. Sitting beside a window in a brightly lit room when we know someone wants to kill you is just carelessness."

She was quiet and seemed to be thinking something over as they plated their food and started to eat. "I have a business to run," she finally said.

Alarmed at where that comment might lead, Luke stopped eating.

"I have to get back to work," she continued. "I don't mean I want to go out of town to sell things. Right now that's the *last* thing I want to do. I can make jewelry at home, but I need to go into The Mercantile and spend some time setting up the furniture I have left so I can sell it. Normally I get out into the community to find old home furnishings to fix up and sell, but I realize under the circumstances it would be smarter to try to buy those things online. I need to get moving on that. The explosion in the storage space ruined all the inventory I had in there."

"All of that can wait," Luke said.

Melanie sighed. "Eventually I'll have the

business set up so I don't need to leave the house if all this drags on for a long time. Meanwhile I have medical bills coming my way. Anna's mortgage payment is still due every month. She and Tyler took out loans to make improvements on the house based on my agreement to move in and pay rent for a couple of years. I've only been there one year. They helped me out when I really needed them. I can't let them down."

Luke nodded and made himself take a bite of food, even though he was starting to lose his appetite. He couldn't tell her what to do. And he couldn't guarantee she'd be completely safe, even if she stayed home and hid under her bed all day long.

"Make sure you always have someone with you," he said. "And don't work alone with Peter. Just to be safe."

She cocked an eyebrow. "Thanks for the marching orders."

He decided to ignore the hint of sarcasm. "You're welcome."

As they ate he thought about the various theories he'd sketched out in his mind regarding who was after her and why. There was one particular topic he needed to pursue, but he wanted to wait until she was finished eating to talk about it.

When it was clear she'd finished her lunch, he set down his own knife and fork, and sat back in his chair. "Tell me about your ex-husband."

"What do you want to know?" she asked in a flat tone.

"I want to take a closer look at him as a suspect. So, first of all, do you know where he is?"

"As far as I know, he still lives in California."

"Do you two have any disputes I should know about? Regarding money, maybe, or property? Did you fight over the division of your assets when you divorced?"

She laughed. Once. And it wasn't a joyful sound. "We were in debt up to our eyeballs in California. After we split up and sold everything, the modest amount of cash remaining was divided in half. I used mine to move home and start my business." She sighed and shook her head. "He's called me a couple of times, asking for money. I told him I had no extra money. That starting a business was an expensive undertaking that didn't necessarily pay off quickly."

"Why would he ask you for money?"

"He probably asked everybody he knew. He tried to get me to feel sorry for him. At this point I hold him no ill will. But I'm also not financially responsible for him. He's a grown man."

"Has he been here in town lately?"

Melanie shrugged. "Maybe. He has family here." She gave him the names of some of her ex-husband's family members and friends.

They cleaned up after their meal, and Luke led the way to the security office. Don was finished with his conference call and, at

Luke's request, was willing to join them in revisiting the areas where Melanie had been found the night of the attack. Having Don along as an extra pair of eyes to scan the area for any hint of trouble as they walked around made Luke feel better.

They started in the vendor area inside the main building, where she would have set up her booth. Don was able to pull up a document that showed precisely the area she had been assigned that night. As Luke already knew, the surveillance video for that area was limited and not of much use.

"Feels odd to be in here alone," Melanie said, her voice echoing off the concrete floor and walls.

"But you aren't alone," Luke said. She glanced at him and flashed him a nervous smile. "I meant without a crowd." She was on edge and he didn't blame her. Even if she couldn't remember all of what had happened, she remembered what had to be one of the most frightening parts.

"Could you recognize the voice of the person who put their hand over your mouth?" Luke asked. "Was it a man or a woman?"

"I don't know. The voice was a whisper. So, if that person spoke to me in a normal voice, I'm not sure I'd recognize them."

Nothing she saw inside the arena triggered a memory, so they went outside.

Looking in the direction of the section of woods where she'd been found, she took a deep breath and squared her shoulders.

Luke couldn't help admiring her. It took courage to do what she was doing right now, returning to the scene of a very traumatic event. And it took strength to hold herself together after three attacks on her life. He knew she was a woman of faith, and he believed he could almost see her leaning into the faith when she needed it.

The way she handled herself was impressive. And knowing these attacks had come on the heels of a divorce she had not asked for, as well as the stress of starting her own business, made her all the more impressive. It gave her a strong presence that could be, well, *soothin*g was the only word he could think of. Not in the way of someone consciously attempting to be reassuring, but in the way of someone who had been through rough times and had been made stronger by the experience. A woman a man could rely on.

Realizing where his thoughts were going, Luke immediately took his eyes off her and scanned their surroundings, instead. He had to keep her safe, so he had to be vigilant. And he had to keep his thoughts professional. He knew what kind of man he was. An adrenaline junkie who would be leaving town in a year or less to pursue that rush. *That* was what had kept him sane and able to deal with all of the tragedies life had thrown at him. He was not husband material and he knew that about himself. He could admire Melanie from an emotional distance. But he would not dwell on it.

He continued to scan their surroundings, keeping an eye out for anybody who looked suspicious, as they walked the area of the parking lot where her truck had been the evening of the attack. Then they continued along the path she'd run all the way to the spot where she'd been lying when he first saw her.

Melanie was quiet as they walked, and Luke didn't say anything, because he didn't want to interrupt her train of thought. Don followed his lead, staying quiet while continually scanning their surroundings. Finally she turned to Luke and shook her head. "I don't remember any more of what happened here. I'm sorry."

"There's no reason for you to apologize," he said as they headed back toward the main building and his parked truck.

Putting any more pressure on Melanie when she was already under enormous stress would not help. So he kept his thoughts to himself as he wondered about the next turn this case would take. It was possible the assailant would leave town before he could be identified. But based on everything that had happened so far, it seemed more likely he would try again to kill her.

Melanie hummed along with the folk music playing throughout the store as she finished arranging a ceramic teapot with a Blue Willow pattern and six matching teacups. Then she stepped back to make sure their placement on the bookshelf visually flowed with the rest of the items in her display area in The Mercantile.

She was glad she'd made the decision to come in to work for a little while today, and especially happy that Diana had agreed to take care of much of Melanie's in-store responsibilities for her until things settled down. She'd meant it when she'd told Luke yesterday that she didn't want to take any unnecessary risks. She just wanted to make sure her business didn't collapse while she spent most of her time hiding at Anna's house.

In the section of floor space she rented in the center of the store, she'd placed a pair of tall, heavy bookcases beside each other, put a couple of hand-braided rugs on the floor in front of them and placed several pieces of furniture she'd refurbished in a nice arrangement beside a locked display case, where she kept her handmade jewelry. Diana had a key, so she could show and sell the jewelry when Melanie wasn't there.

"Dwayne brought cupcakes!" Diana called out in a singsong voice as she sailed past.

Melanie glanced over her shoulder to see Diana carrying a clear plastic bakery tray with a dozen frosted cupcakes inside. Dwayne walked behind her, smiling broadly and carrying a stack of colorful advertisements of some sort.

Rodeos were winding down for the season, but Dwayne would have something going on. He always did. Maybe a big swap meet or a Western art show. Back in the day he'd been quite the rodeo star on the national level. When that was over he'd invested his money in his own business, which involved organizing amateur rodeos, ranch liquidation sales, swap meets and all kinds of things.

The man was a natural born promoter. He had a paid staff to take care of most of the details of his various enterprises, but he was smart enough to know if he came by in person, bearing delicious treats, Diana and everyone associated with The Mercantile would talk up whatever upcoming event he had and help his business.

"Come on back to the office with us and have a cupcake," Diana said to Melanie as she walked by. "It's almost closing time. Take a break. I'll put on a pot of decaf."

Dwayne slowed down to talk to Melanie. "I'm so sorry to hear about what's been happening to you," he said. "I hope they catch whoever it is. And soon."

"Thank you." Even though she'd talked to him several times, including rebuffing his multiple offers to buy into her jewelry business and help expand it, it was still a little strange to see him in person. He used his former rodeo-star status to boost sales, starring in his own TV commercials and plastering his face on all of his advertisements.

It was obvious he dyed his hair black, and the skin around his eyes looked unnaturally tight for a man in his mid-fifties. Maybe he'd gotten a facelift so he'd look better on TV.

"If there's anything I can do to help you, please let me know," he said.

"I will."

He headed back toward the office and she found herself wondering about Dwayne's relationship with Diana. Just like she'd begun to wonder about so many things after someone started trying to kill her. Not because she was interested in gossip, but because she needed to pay attention. People had secrets, worries that might push them to desperation, and they did things under pressure that they would normally never do. Maybe something like that had triggered the attacks on Melanie.

Diana, she knew, did not own The Mercantile outright, even though her grandparents had gifted it to her. She'd had to take out loans for some substantial repairs to the old building. She also liked to go to the casinos and play cards. She'd won big a few times, but she'd lost even bigger. Money was a source of worry for Diana; she kept no secret of that. Dwayne had money and was always looking for a way to expand his commercial empire. Maybe he'd invested in The Mercantile and become a silent partner. Maybe that was part of the reason why he came by the store so often.

Melanie shook off the thought. Whatever was going on with either of them was none of her business. There was nothing to be gained by letting her imagination work overtime. She was just nervous and tired, and she wished her life could go back to normal.

From the office she could hear Peter and one of the store's other employees burst into what sounded like sugar-fueled laughter. Any other time she would have been first in line to enjoy a little social time and a cupcake, but if she went back there to join in the fun right now, they'd see the weight on her shoulders and the heaviness in her heart. How could they miss it?

And they'd see the fear. Much as she tried not to focus on the fear, it was always there. Making her stomach queasy. And making her feel like her nerves had been electrified and there was no way for her to ground them.

"Have a good night," Dwayne called out as he walked by, and Melanie nearly jumped out of her skin.

"You're not staying to eat cupcakes?" she asked, trying to sound relaxed and normal.

"Nah. I'm flying down to Denver tonight,"

he said as he kept walking. "There's a storm rolling through later and I want to take off before it gets here."

He kept a private plane at the regional airport.

She glanced at her phone and saw that it was just about time for The Mercantile to close up. She called Anna on her phone, asking her to come get her.

Everyone who'd been in the office started to drift back out into the store. She knew Peter would go outside to retrieve the sandwich sign on the sidewalk and clean up a little out there before they locked up. One of the sales clerks would clock out and head for home, while the other would help Diana take care of the day's financial records in her office. For security's sake the procedure was to have at least three people at the store who would all walk out together when they locked up. Knowing there would be other people around was part of the reason why Melanie felt reasonably safe being here.

The overhead lights turned off. It must be exactly eight o'clock now. The folk music continued to play throughout the store. Diana usually left that on until everybody was ready to head out the door.

There was enough ambient light from the streetlamps outside the windows for Melanie to see what she was doing as she reached over to put away some cleaning supplies she'd been using. As she straightened, she felt a brush of air across her cheek and turned just in time to see the glint of a sharply pointed blade at the end of a long knife headed straight for the base of her throat.

She was so scared, she couldn't draw in enough of a breath to scream.

Sheer instinct made her throw out her arm in an attempt to knock away the knife. She felt the razor edge of the blade slice through the flesh on her lower arm before hearing the knife clatter to the floor.

The attacker threw something over her

head, blinding her. It was the same technique he'd used outside the coffee shop.

Overwhelming fear sent her heart racing, while terror-fueled panic gave her a burst of energy. She flailed her arms, trying to strike the attacker, who was behind her, but couldn't make her fists connect with his body. Meanwhile he kept control of her by tightening his grip on the towel or blanket or whatever it was he'd thrown over her head.

She finally forced out a scream, using every bit of air in her lungs, but it came out sounding muffled. And then, when she tried to take another breath, the fabric that was pulled tightly across her face was drawn into her mouth. She got some air, but not much. She started to feel light-headed. Her pulse thundered in her ears. If she passed out, it would be easy for him to kill her.

Dear Lord, help!

Why was no one coming to her aid?

Everyone had gone off in different directions, finishing up their last tasks of the night. That was why. And they probably couldn't hear her over the music playing throughout the store.

Noise. She needed to make a lot of noise.

Fearful that the sleepy, detached feeling creeping into her consciousness meant that she was about to pass out, she put every last bit of strength she had into balancing on one leg and then kicking with the other. She swung her arms all around, too. Not just behind her, toward the attacker, but in every direction, trying to knock something over.

She threw all of her weight into lunging forward, and she managed to hit something that knocked over something else, sending it to the floor with a loud clatter.

Then she bent both of her knees, pulling her feet up off the ground. The weight of her body pulled her from the attacker's grip and she fell forward, hard. Barely feeling the pain, she rolled around on the ground, with her face still covered by the cloth, frantically trying to knock something over so she could make more noise.

Her attempts were working. There was more clattering, more things falling over. Fighting for her breath, she finally got to her hands and knees and tried to crawl away, wanting desperately to pull the cloth off her head but afraid that would slow her down.

She bumped her head against something and then her way was blocked. It felt like one of her bookcases. She was trapped. She had no choice but to take the time to pull the cloth off her head so she could see where she was going. But just as she did, the bookshelf toppled over onto her.

The music in the store stopped. "Melanie, are you all right?" she heard Ginny, the sales clerk who'd stayed to help Diana, call out from the office area.

And then she heard the sound of footsteps running away.

"Help!" Melanie yelled, moving the bookcase that was lying on top of her a little bit and finally able to take a deep breath. The struggle with the attacker had probably lasted only a couple of minutes, but it felt like it had lasted forever.

The fire alarm started blaring. It was connected to the exit at the back of the store. The attacker must have run out that way.

The store lights came on and Ginny ran toward Melanie, with her phone up to her ear. "It's going to be okay," she said to Melanie. She tucked the phone between her ear and her shoulder as she tried to lift the bookcase off Melanie while talking to the 9-1-1 operator.

No, it's not going to be okay, Melanie thought, still fighting to catch her breath as she looked at the blood from the cut on her arm that had spilled all over the floor. The attacker was relentless. And the cops were no closer to capturing him.

SEVEN

Over the scanner in the sheriff's department headquarters, Luke heard a 9-1-1 operator dispatch a fire engine in response to an alarm at The Mercantile. He was out of his chair and heading to his truck in a heartbeat, aware that Melanie was working a few hours there today. She might have already left for home and forgotten to let him know, but he was not taking any chances.

Inside his truck he started the engine and used the hands-free device to call her number. She didn't pick up and the call rolled over to voice mail. His already rapid heartbeat began to pound even harder. He flipped on his lights and sirens and said a prayer as he shot down the road.

The fire engine and ambulance took up the space directly in front of the store, so he drove past them and parked down the block. He got out and jogged toward the red brick building that housed The Mercantile, desperate to see Melanie and confirm for himself that she was all right.

Cold fear for her safety knotted his stomach, while hot anger swirled over the surface of his skin at the thought that the assailant might have attacked her again. He didn't yet know what had happened, but he imagined the worst and was already making plans for how he would respond. That was how he'd done his job in the military, and now as a deputy. It was how he'd learned to live his life. Be prepared for the worst. Have a plan. Keep a lid on his emotions.

"False alarm," a firefighter standing outside the building called out to Luke as he jogged up. "Nothing's burning."

Luke had already noticed a lack of flames or smoke, but that didn't mean Melanie wasn't in danger. Maybe she'd triggered the alarm as a signal that she needed help. He didn't slow down until he reached the front door, yanked it open and hurried inside.

Diana stood near the entrance, arms crossed over her chest, looking around like she was afraid someone would use the diversion of the arrival of all the emergency responders to rob her store. Peter Altman, his face like a pale, blank mask, stood beside a woman Luke didn't recognize. She wore a name tag declaring her name was Ginny. She turned toward Luke, and her eyes were wide with fear. "Melanie?" he shouted.

Visibly trembling, she pointed toward the center of the building, where Melanie's display area was located. At the same time, a patrol officer from the Bowen Police Department walked through the front door. "See that nobody leaves the building other than emergency personnel," Luke said to him.

Maybe Peter and Ginny looked scared because they couldn't believe what had just happened. Or maybe they were involved in something and they were scared they'd get caught. At the moment Luke was suspicious of everybody and he didn't want anyone leaving until they'd all been interviewed. He didn't know for certain yet if what had just happened to Melanie was connected to the attacks on her, but for now he was assuming the worst.

He hurried to the center of the store and saw Melanie sitting in a chair, with a paramedic applying some kind of ointment to her lower left arm and getting ready to wrap it with a white bandage. She was talking and was apparently all right, except for the injury on her arm.

Luke took a deep breath and exhaled. *Thank You, Lord.*

She glanced in his direction, her gaze lingering on him while she answered the paramedic's questions. Luke wanted to smile encouragingly at her, reassure her, but he couldn't. He would not lie to her. Until he had the assailant locked up, she was in danger.

"He came after me. Here, in the store," Melanie said, her voice shaky with fear and strained by the obvious effort it took for her to hold back tears. Despite her effort, a tear escaped. Luke watched it roll down her cheek and he felt like his heart was breaking in two.

She lifted her chin, and a trembling smile formed on her lips. "I fought him off, though," she said.

Her courage was impressive. And it made Luke's heart ache even more. She was not a trained fighter, but she nevertheless did not give up.

The paramedic indicated that he needed Melanie's attention turned back to him for the moment. Luke would have to wait a little longer for the specific details. Meanwhile he could hear the sounds of other cops walking into the building, including intermittent transmissions over their law-enforcement radios.

While the medic attended to Melanie, he looked around her merchandising area and saw several splatters of blood near her jewelry display case. Maybe some of that blood belonged to the assailant. He would have the forensic techs gather samples. It could help with getting a conviction once he had his prime suspect. Of course he'd also have them check for prints, and he'd look at security footage—whatever Diana had for the store, plus any outside video recorded by other businesses on the street.

He looked around a little more. A heavy bookcase was toppled over and cracked on one side. Several other items made of glass or ceramic were also broken. Some of the small pieces of furniture were also knocked on their sides and damaged. He knew they were just things, that they could be replaced. But taken together, they represented a dream Melanie had put her time and energy into.

Likewise someone might argue that his family ranch was just land and buildings and animals that could be replaced, but to both him and Jake it was much more than that. It was home, and it was also an emotional anchor in their lives. A place of reliability when the world turned chaotic.

The forensic techs arrived and Luke talked to them. Then he directed the Bowen city cops who'd shown up to individually interview each of the store employees and get a timeline for where they'd been during the attack.

There was a commotion near the front entrance, and seconds later Anna burst into view, hurrying toward Melanie and reaching out to give her cousin a hug.

"What happened? Are you all right?" The words spilled out of Anna's mouth almost without a break between them.

Luke gestured to one of the cops and then nodded toward Anna. While he could empathize with Anna's horror at seeing her cousin attacked yet again, he was also determined to be the first person to hear Melanie's description of what had happened before her recollection could be influenced by anyone else's questions or comments.

"I'm sorry I took so long to get here," Anna called to Melanie as the police officer politely led her away. "I stopped by Casa Victoria to get tamales for dinner."

"It's all right," Melanie said.

Luke would have the cops get Anna's timeline for the last hour, just like they were doing with the store employees. He had no reason to suspect her of anything, but he still wanted to know where she was and whom she might have been talking to. Maybe she'd unthinkingly told somebody that Melanie was working at The Mercantile tonight.

Luke was determined to cast a wide net to find his suspect. One of his fellow deputies with family in eastern Montana had told him about a local news story related to her by her sister who lived over there.

A woman had been seriously injured by an explosive device placed outside her home. That piece of information had started Luke thinking about the explosion at Melanie's storage space. Maybe the incidents were related. Maybe the assailant who kept coming after Melanie had targeted other women in the past.

He'd already started checking with law enforcement agencies in other counties in Idaho, as well as the FBI, to see if there were any other similarities between what had happened to Melanie and crimes close by or in other states. The responses were pending.

Luke was desperate to keep her safe, but there were limits to what his sheriff's department could do. It would be ideal if he could hide her away somewhere, but even then there would be no guarantee that the attacker wouldn't find her. At least here, in Bowen, she had people looking after her who cared about her. She had *him*. The only reason he hadn't been here with her this evening was because both he and the sheriff thought she'd be safe with her coworkers around her. And Luke had other responsibilities at department headquarters that he'd needed to get caught up on.

The paramedic suggested Melanie go by the hospital to have her cut arm examined and offered to transport her. She agreed to go, but she didn't want to be transported by ambulance. Luke offered to take her. He could get her description of what had happened at the same time.

During the drive Melanie recounted what had happened in an emotionless voice that told him she was probably in shock. He listened with a calm demeanor, though inside he was furious and wishing he'd been at The Mercantile to deal with the attacker himself.

At the hospital, while she was being treated by a doctor, Luke called the city cops for an update. None of the employees' explanations of their whereabouts just prior to the attack seemed suspicious.

Since the cops were still at the scene, Luke asked them to talk to the employees about who they'd seen in or around the store earlier today. The assailant must have known the routine for closing time at the store. He'd timed his attack precisely. He must have been in the store before. Or he'd talked to somebody who worked there. Someone at The Mercantile had seen or talked to the assailant. But they might not have realized it.

He thought about Peter and his brothers, who were already on Luke's list of possible suspects.

Melanie had mentioned Dwayne Skinner's stopping by. Luke had asked if Dwayne had acted strangely or if there was any bad blood between the two of them, and Melanie had answered no on both accounts. Following up on what she'd told him, Luke called out to the regional airport where Dwayne kept his private plane. His contact confirmed that Dwayne had filed a flight plan for Denver and had taken off roughly forty minutes after the attack at The Mercantile. In theory he could have pretended to leave after dropping off the posters and cupcakes, waited around, attacked Melanie and then raced out to the airport. But why?

He had no motive for Dwayne to attack Melanie, but he would still add him to the list of possible suspects and keep him there until he could rule him out.

Having done all he could for the moment, and still waiting for Melanie, Luke turned his attention to something he'd been considering doing for the last couple of days. Now might be the time to act on it. He reached for his phone. He had a call to make.

"Wow, the rain really is coming down hard." Melanie stood at the edge of the covered walkway outside the hospital, where the headlights on Luke's idling truck made the falling raindrops in front of them sparkle like diamonds.

"Yeah." Luke nodded. A few raindrops

clung to the brim of his cowboy hat and danced when he moved his head. "Unfortunately the brunt of the storm is overhead right now, just when it's time for you to leave."

Her whole body hurt from her battle with the bad guy in The Mercantile. Except for her lower left arm, which was numb. The doctor had cleaned the five-inch cut and sewn it up with sutures that would eventually dissolve on their own.

After the sheer terror of the attack in the store, she'd become wrapped in a feeling of detachment. It felt like it had all happened to someone else. She'd reached the limit of what she could emotionally process.

But somewhere between dealing with the various people she interacted with in the hospital and sitting alone on a cold chair, waiting for the next step in the process of getting taken care of, the feeling of detachment had started to slip away. She'd found herself whispering, *Thank You, Lord, for keeping me alive*, several times over.

She realized that that feeling of raw terror that had coursed through her during the attack could come roaring back at any minute, and at that moment she could choose to dwell on what might have happened, or she could be grateful for what *did* happen. She'd fought off an evil person who'd meant to kill her. She'd *survived*.

With that thought in mind—the idea that she could choose how she saw things—the raindrops were beautiful. The chilly breeze was refreshing. The rumbling sound of Luke's truck, which was there to take her home, was reassuring.

Luke was reassuring. And she was amazed that he'd stayed at the hospital the whole time. They'd been there a couple of hours. He could have taken care of other responsibilities at work during that time. Or relaxed at home. It was late. It was possible he was here with her now on his own time.

He'd been a soldier and was now a deputy. He'd come back to Idaho to help his brother. He'd helped her. In a world where it seemed only natural to keep an eye out for yourself and what you could get, he was a man looking to give and to help. It was impossible not to admire that.

A little alarm went off in the back of her mind. Warning her to protect her heart. This man wanted excitement, not domestic bliss in Bowen. And she wanted a man who was inclined to talk about his feelings, something Luke didn't do so much. Actually she didn't even want a man in her life. Not right now, when she had a business to build. And she was not inclined to date just for fun. At some point she'd be ready to look for a husband and plan for the future, but not right now. Right now she needed to focus on staying alive.

Luke helped her up into his truck, and then walked around to the driver's side and climbed in.

Melanie was determined to soak up the sense of security she felt with him so near to her. At some point later tonight, when she was trying to sleep, a feeling of security would be hard to come by. Recent experience had shown her that old tormentor, fear, would likely keep her awake until dawn.

She was surprised when Luke drove only a few feet away from the hospital entrance and pulled into one of the empty slots in the hospital parking lot. He put the truck into Park and then turned to her. For a few seconds there was only the sound of the wipers slapping back and forth across the windshield. Then he said, "I called Anna and asked if she'd had an alarm system installed at the house, like I suggested. She said she'd ordered one, but that it wasn't installed yet."

"That's right," Melanie said. "I told her I'd pay for it, since it was mainly for my benefit. Gem Mountain Security is supposed to install it tomorrow."

"I'd like you to stay at my family's ranch

tonight. Maybe even a couple of days beyond that. As long as it takes to get the security system installed."

Melanie didn't know which shocked her more. His belief that the attacker might come after her again later tonight, or his willingness to invite her into his home.

"I don't want Anna to be alone," she said, her surprise making her fumble over the words.

"I invited her to come to the ranch, as well. She said she hadn't spent as much time with her in-laws as she should have lately and she'd rather stay with them, instead."

Melanie thought it over for a moment. "In that case I guess going to the ranch is a good idea. I just need to go by the house and get some clothes."

"Of course." He backed out of the parking slot and headed toward the road.

"We should probably get a dog for the house for extra security," Melanie said, thinking out loud.

"Good idea. We've got a spoiled, untrainable mutt at the ranch you could have."

She glanced over at him. The smile on his face told her he was joking.

Forty minutes later she was outside the house, hugging Anna goodbye before they went their separate ways. It was only going to be one night. Maybe two. But given the relentlessness of the assailant targeting her, Melanie gave Anna an extra-tight squeeze. And then the cousins both started to sniffle and make fun of each other for crying.

"Enough," Luke said, looking at Melanie and sounding serious but not unkind. "Standing out here is the worst possible thing you could do right now. It makes you an easy target."

Melanie got into the truck and they drove away. Luke repeatedly glanced at the rear-view mirror as they wound along the curving mountain roads, heading east for a little while and then north, with the road rising higher in elevation the farther they went. A couple of times, when there was a break in the thick forest alongside the highway, Luke pulled over and waited.

"Are you trying to see if anyone is following us?" Melanie asked the first time he did it.

Luke had kept his gaze locked on the side mirror and nodded his head *yes*.

Feeling more anxious as they drove farther into the dark wilderness outside of town, Melanie chattered nervously about a variety of topics, from freeway gridlock in California to the ridiculous lack of realism in old TV cop shows. Luke didn't add anything to the conversation, but then she never really gave him the chance.

She talked when she was nervous. And apparently he got very quiet when he was nervous. And vigilant. She wasn't sure if their opposite reactions were a good thing or a bad thing, but really what did it matter? They were heading out of town to keep her alive. They were not on a date.

A few minutes later he slowed down and turned off the highway, onto a narrow dirt road. He immediately pulled off to the side of that road, onto a patch of grass, lowered his window, then turned off the headlights and cut the engine. Once again his attention was focused on the side mirror.

"You're still watching to see if anyone followed us," she said.

"And listening for the same reason. Someone following us might have pulled over when I turned onto the drive. If they knew what they were doing, they'd move forward on foot to see if I'd set a trap." Which apparently he had. And she should probably stop talking.

He gave it a few minutes, and after nothing happened he reached for his phone and tapped the screen. "We just turned off the road," he said when someone answered his call. "Be there in a few seconds."

He started up the engine and followed the long drive until the trees began to thin and split-rail fences came into sight, marking the boundaries of grassy meadows. The ground was hilly and the drive approached the ranch house at an angle.

The house appeared to be a single-story building, crowning a hill at the entrance, but as they moved forward she could see it in fact had a second story below, on the downslope side. Outside that floor was an expansive patio, and beyond that she could see a barn, stables, a few other outbuildings and a corral. The night was dark and rain was still coming down, but the outside lighting attached to the various buildings let her see enough to know this was a working ranch and not simply a home in the country with some acreage.

"Do you raise horses here?" she asked.

"American quarter horses," he said. "And Appaloosas. No championship lineages or anything like that. Just strong, solid animals who are happy to be around people, cattle, dogs and the occasional barn cat."

Luke parked by the front door, grabbed

Melanie's suitcase from the back seat and then came around to help her out. Having her arm numb made it harder to deal with unfastening her seat belt and climbing out than she would have imagined.

He opened the front door of the house and the warmth that greeted them felt like a hug.

A man who favored Luke, but with a slightly smaller frame and lighter-colored hair, stepped into the foyer. "I'm Jake," he said, extending a hand to Melanie. "Welcome."

"I'm sorry to barge in on you like this," Melanie said after introducing herself. She could smell the faint, lingering scent of something savory and delicious.

"People barge in here all the time," another voice called out. A wiry man and a woman with her thick blond hair tied into a braid walked into the foyer behind Jake.

Jake smiled broadly. "That's true. Meet my late wife's brother, Steven, and his wife, Tanya."

"Nice to meet you," Melanie said.

Steven smiled at her, nodded and then turned to Luke. "Jake invited us over for dinner earlier this evening. We were still here when you called your brother and told him what happened at The Mercantile tonight and that you'd be bringing home a guest. We decided to stay here tonight, too. Just in case there was trouble."

Melanie didn't know what to say. She was embarrassed to inconvenience so many people. And grateful for their help.

Jake started to lead the way toward the living room when an animal appeared, and for a moment Melanie wasn't quite sure what she was looking at. Its fur was black and brown, and long, except for the spots where it was completely missing. One ear stood up, while the other flopped down, and it had a pair of amazingly bushy eyebrows. About the time Melanie figured out it was a dog, it started to wag its tail.

"Meet Billy Clyde," Luke said.

Melanie knelt down and reached out to

scratch the dog on the head, and his tail wagged twice as hard.

"Uncle Luke."

Melanie glanced up and saw a sleepy-eyed little boy, maybe six or seven years old, in fuzzy blue pajamas, rubbing his eyes and walking down a hallway toward them. She got to her feet.

"Hey, little man," Luke called out to him. "Shouldn't you be in bed?"

"Yes," Jake said sternly, though the expression on his face was soft as he looked at his son.

There was a shuffling sound in the hallway and now a second child headed toward them. This time it was a little girl, a year or two younger than the boy.

"Hey, Kayla," Luke said as she drew closer.

Melanie inwardly cringed at the realization that the noise and commotion caused by her arrival with Luke must have woken the children. She glanced at Luke. He smiled at the kids and threw his arms open wide.

The boy made a beeline straight toward him. The girl caught up a few seconds later. Their dad sighed heavily and rolled his eyes. But then the corners of his mouth lifted in a resigned grin.

Both kids claimed their own side of their uncle as he squatted down and wrapped an arm around each of them. They pressed their faces to his neck, and Luke closed his eyes and smiled. Slowly his smile faded. He kept his eyes closed for a few more seconds, his face more relaxed than Melanie had ever seen it.

He had to recognize the impact those children had on him. Or was he in such deep denial that he truly believed he would let his drive to chase after the next adrenaline rush take him away from them and from his family home?

He opened his eyes and released the kids. Melanie decided he was probably like a lot of people. Like she had been for a stretch of her life. He would chase after the thing that would never really fulfill him. Eventually he'd figure out his mistake. Probably. But that would be in the future. Most likely in another town. Maybe even in another country. In any event she wouldn't be around to see it.

Luke made the introductions between Melanie and his niece and nephew. Both children smiled shyly at her. With Luke's encouragement, Alan stepped up to shake her hand. Then Kayla copied her brother.

"I've got some leftover homemade turkey potpie I can reheat for you and Luke," Jake said to Melanie after he gave each of his kids a kiss on the top of their heads. "Let me show you to your room right now and you can rest for a few minutes while I get the kids settled back in their beds, and then I'll get your food ready."

"You go ahead and take care of Kayla and Alan," Tanya said, stepping forward. She picked up Melanie's suitcase from the spot on the floor where Luke had set it down and turned to Melanie, smiling. "I'll help you get settled in."

Tanya led her to a room that was spacious and had its own private bathroom. There was a dresser with a mirror, and when Melanie caught sight of herself, she brought her right hand up to her cheek. Her skin was pale except for the dark purple circles under her eyes, and thanks to the stormy weather, the walk from Luke's truck to the ranch house had left her hair practically standing on end. At least she'd changed into clean clothes when she'd gone home to pack her bag. Too bad she hadn't thought to touch up her makeup, but at the time that had been the farthest thing from her mind. Instead, her thoughts had been focused on the lingering emotional shock of having been attacked. Again.

Tanya moved around the room, pulling an extra blanket from the closet and setting it on the foot of the bed. She checked the lock on the window and made sure the curtains were completely closed. Then she fetched some bath towels and placed them on the bathroom counter.

All the while Melanie stood, looking at her reflection and thinking about what had happened to her tonight.

Finally she collected herself before she fell any farther into that rabbit hole of fear. "Thank you," she said to Tanya in a soft voice, because she was suddenly very tired. "Sorry for the trouble."

"It's no trouble," Tanya said, looking a little self-conscious and fiddling with the blond braid that hung over her shoulder. "We're all happy to help you. And we're happy to do this for Luke. He's done so much for all of us. Coming back after Janelle passed away, being a strong support for his brother. And for my husband, too. Janelle was Steven's only sibling."

Melanie nodded. Luke had told her a little about his late sister-in-law, and she realized what a tragic loss her passing was for the family.

Tanya brought her hands together. "So, I'm going to head to the kitchen. You take as much time as you need in here, then come get something to eat." She turned and left.

Melanie went into the bathroom to wash her hands and fix her hair. Then she left her room and went in search of the kitchen. She was determined to help out and be good company while she was with Luke's family. It was the only way she knew how to repay their kindness. Not many people would help protect a complete stranger from a potential killer.

EIGHT

Luke stared into the darkness. He'd been lying in bed for about five hours. It was nearing 4:00 a.m. Maybe he'd slept a little; he wasn't sure. He only knew that he'd been mentally reviewing everything Melanie had told him about the attack at The Mercantile last night. After that his thoughts had taken him back to what he knew about the explosion at her storage space. Then back to the attack outside the coffee shop. And then back to the initial attempt on her life at the rodeo grounds.

Once he'd thought through it all, picturing the situations, figuring out where his suspects were at the time of each attack, working out possible motives, he'd done it all again. And again.

His suspect list felt thin. It was simply a collection of all the people Melanie regularly came into contact with. He had no clues to point him toward anyone else. Sadly a lot of murders, assaults and robberies were committed by perpetrators known to the victim. And at the other end of the spectrum, the assailant could be some psychopath who randomly chose her as his victim. But if that were the case, Luke would have no way of figuring out who the psychopath was based on the information he had. So he'd turned his thoughts back to her friends, family and coworkers.

And wondered, for what felt like the millionth time, how anyone who knew Melanie could want to do her harm. He had to keep her safe. He had to find out who was attacking her and bring that person to justice. And then he and Melanie would go back to living their lives.

Jake and the kids were great, but Jake's kind of life was not Luke's kind of life. He'd figured that out a long time ago. He loved them, but he still felt restless every now and then. Edgy and itching for something more exciting. He wasn't ready to settle down. Not even close to ready.

Maybe he'd let his emotions get tangled up in this case with Melanie. He'd let his thoughts cross the line and he'd momentarily considered a possible relationship with her in the future. But then he'd acknowledged the futility of that and hopped back across that line. He was a public servant. She was a citizen in danger. That was all.

Except she was in his house. Which was bugging him right now, because it felt like she was way too close. Yet at the same time he didn't want her to go anywhere else. He wanted her here, with him, where he and his brother and their friends could keep her safe.

Luke looked at the bedside clock. It was 4:15 a.m. He flung off the covers, got out of bed and got ready for the day. He decided to brew some coffee and then head to the office to see what new leads he could drum up on this case.

The last few drops of coffee were gurgling into the carafe of the coffee maker when he heard shuffling footsteps. Melanie walked into the kitchen, bumping into the side of the doorway on her way in.

She wore the same clothes she'd had on last night at dinner. Only now they were rumpled and wrinkly. It looked like she'd worn them to bed. And while she might have gone to bed, it didn't look like she'd gotten much sleep. The dark circles she'd had under her eyes last night were, remarkably, even darker this morning. Her hair stuck out in every direction. And she looked like she was on the verge of bursting into tears.

Luke wanted to wrap his arms around her, hold her close and tell her things would get better. But he couldn't do that. Because he wasn't really a "hang around forever" guy.

He was a "head into the battle, bust down the door, catch the criminal and then leave" guy. And sending a woman misleading signals was not the way he rolled.

He stood with the small of his back pressed against the edge of the countertop, watching her closely. "You're up early," he said.

She rubbed her eyes. "I couldn't sleep."

"Your room's not comfortable?"

"It isn't that." She pulled out a chair at the kitchen table and plopped down into it. "My mind keeps racing. And my arm hurts."

She'd been through a lot of trauma over the last few days. It made sense that she couldn't quiet her mind enough to fall asleep. "Did you take the pain pills the doctor gave you?"

"No. I don't want to be sedated. What if the bad guy comes back?"

"Here?" Luke said. "You have people looking out for you here. And Billy Clyde would bark up a storm if anyone came around."

Billy Clyde either recognized his name or just heard voices and wanted to know what was going on. He padded into the kitchen and sat down on the floor, beside Melanie. She reached over and rubbed his ears.

"The house and stables are set up with a security system," Luke added, hoping to help her feel as safe as possible. Of course the reality was that, if the attacker was determined to get to her no matter the cost, alarms and lights wouldn't keep him away.

"Did you make that entire pot of coffee just for yourself?" Melanie asked, gazing longingly at it.

"Nope." He filled a mug halfway with coffee, finished it with milk and handed it to her. Maybe she'd eventually be able to fall asleep if she didn't get too caffeinated. She took a sip and didn't complain. That was good. He drank his own coffee black.

"I feel like I now remember that whole two-week timespan I'd lost after the attack," Melanie said quietly. "That was a lot of what was running through my mind all night. Thinking about those two weeks."

Luke straightened. "Do you remember anything about the attacker?"

"No." She sighed and her shoulders dropped. "And I'm so disappointed." Her voice started to tremble. "I really thought once my memory came back, I would know who was trying to kill me. But I don't. I remember the person at the fairgrounds coming up behind me and shoving a gun into my neck. But I never saw him. He spoke in a whisper so I couldn't recognize his voice."

"Can you remember anything unusual during those two weeks? Or even before. I know you never lost your memory of being at that rodeo in Wyoming, but I can't help thinking that maybe something happened there that triggered the attacks."

"No," she said, shaking her head. "I can't."

That was disappointing. Like her, he had hoped when her memory came back she'd be able to tell him who'd attacked her. Or at least tell him about a specific threat, an altercation, *something* that had led to all of this.

Jake walked into the kitchen, greeted Luke and Melanie, and then made a beeline for the coffee. Steven and Tanya weren't too far behind him.

Now that the others were here to keep Melanie company, Luke filled a travel mug with coffee and grabbed his keys from the countertop. "I'm heading into the office to look over the evidence we have from the attack last night and see what kind of leads we can develop."

"Let me know what you find out," Melanie said tiredly.

"I will." Luke walked past her and was struck by an impulse to lean down and kiss her cheek. He settled for squeezing her shoulder, instead. When she reached up to pat his hand, he felt a wave of emotion that was unnerving. It was a feeling of connection. Like they'd known each other for a long time, instead of just for a few days.

As he left the house he was determined to get his focus back on Melanie's case. And equally determined to lose any personal feelings he had for her.

Late that afternoon, Melanie looked out the front-room window at the lingering slim band of light cast by the setting sun.

Of course she didn't stand too close to the picture window. Tanya had cautioned her about that. As if Melanie could possibly forget her life was in danger.

Tanya was a kind woman. And she'd been good company during the few hours of the day when Melanie had been awake. Surprisingly Melanie had been able to go to sleep after her early morning talk with Luke. Maybe she'd just needed to tell someone about her worries. Or maybe she needed to see Luke's reaction when she told him that even with her memory fully recovered, she couldn't tell him who was trying to kill her.

He didn't give up hope or seem overwhelmed. Instead he seemed like he would simply continue the steady pace of his investigation without breaking stride. Seeing that was very reassuring.

Outside, shadows pooled beneath the pine trees and alongside the buildings and fences. She would be spending a second night here. Anna had called and said the alarm-system installation wouldn't be completed until late afternoon, so why not wait another day to go home.

Staying another night didn't seem like such a bad thing. Especially with the scent of made-from-scratch chicken and dumplings wafting through the house.

Luke had sent her a text a short while ago, saying he was heading back to the ranch and that he had some news for her. She'd immediately sent a text, asking if it was good news. He hadn't replied. Which in her mind meant the answer was no.

So she'd spent some time in prayer and trying to center her emotions. She was as ready as she could be to hear what he had to say and determined to deal with it head-on.

Allowing worry and fear to break her down was not an option. This morning was a reminder of how quickly she could fall apart if she gave into despair. Fighting against hopelessness was a tough battle, but giving into it didn't make things easier.

Her phone chimed with a group text from Luke to all of the adults in the house.

Turning onto the driveway. Vehicle and headlights you see will be me.

Seconds later she saw the headlights and then the big pickup truck. Her stomach knotted in anticipation of hearing the news he had to tell her. She also felt a fluttering sensation in her chest in anticipation of seeing him again. She told herself to ignore it.

Billy Clyde raced to the front door, wagging his tail and giving a couple of joyful barks just before Luke opened it. Alan and Kayla were right behind him. Luke walked through the door, dropped down and extended his arms so the kids could hug him, and then he stood, picking them both up at the same time. And just like last night, the smile on his face when he had the kids in his arms was huge.

No wonder. His niece and nephew were loving and fun to be around. They'd gone to school for part of the day, but they'd been so rambunctious when they came home that they'd accidentally woken Melanie. Which was a good thing, because playing with them had been fun and it had taken her mind off her troubles for a while.

Looking at Luke as he set the children back on their feet, she wondered if he would truly trade the life he had here for the pursuit of thrills in a dangerous occupation somewhere else. Maybe. He'd said as much. And he would know.

He gave each kid a final squeeze and offered Billy Clyde a scratch on the head. Then he stood and glanced in Melanie's direction. She raised her eyebrows in what she hoped was a clearly questioning gesture. She wanted to know what new information he had about the attacker. Wondering about Luke's future, not to mention her own, didn't have much relevance if the assailant launched another attack in the upcoming days and was finally successful.

He nodded toward the kids and she knew he didn't want to talk in front of them. That was understandable. And the somber expression that had returned to his face as his smile faded told her what she'd already guessed. The news he had to share was not good.

They made their way into the kitchen, where Tanya stood by the oven, with her phone in hand. She glanced up and said she'd just texted Jake and Steven to let them know dinner was ready. Both men showed up a short time later, a little bit dusty and smelling like hay. Jake herded his giggling offspring into the hall bathroom so they could all wash their hands. Tanya gathered plates from a cabinet and set them on the counter next to the stove. Melanie had offered her help earlier, but Tanya had politely declined, telling Melanie she needed to rest.

"How's your arm?" Luke asked when it looked like they'd have a minute or two to themselves before everyone sat down to eat.

"It doesn't hurt as much. What's your news?"

He took a deep breath and blew it out. "It's looking like you're not the only person the attacker has tried to kill."

Melanie's heart began to beat double-time. "What are you saying? Did he attack someone else today? Someone here in town?" Immediately she thought of her cousin. And then her associates at The Mercantile. "Anna?" she asked. *Please Lord, let her be all right.* "Did something happen to Anna?" Panic clawed at her throat.

"No. There has not been another attack in town. But there might be a pattern with attacks on women in other Western states over the last eighteen months. Specifically in Montana and Wyoming. The most recent assault happened four months ago."

"Were the women killed?" she asked, feeling a chill sweep through her body and settle into her bones.

"There is one woman that we know of who was murdered, and there could possibly be a link to what has been happening to you. Two others were assaulted. One of them was kidnapped, locked up and left for dead. She was found before it was too late, but she couldn't identify her attacker."

What was he telling her? That there was a serial assaulter, a *serial killer*, who'd set his sights on Melanie? But why her?

"What's the link that you think connects the attacks on me to what happened to those other women?" Melanie asked.

Before Luke could answer, Kayla and Alan ran, squealing, down the hallway, toward the kitchen, with their dad chasing after them.

Everyone was gathering in the kitchen to plate up their dinner and then move to the dining room, where Tanya had already set water glasses and cutlery. Luke's brother and their family friends had worked hard to make Melanie feel at home and to keep the mood as lighthearted as possible, while still remaining vigilant. She realized most of that effort was for the sake of the kids, but she appreciated it, nonetheless.

She was determined to go into dinner right now and make conversation. She would do her best to eat something, even though her stomach felt frozen with fear. Afterward she would talk to Luke privately and have him tell her everything. She drew in as deep a breath as she could and said, "Dinner smells wonderful."

"Feel free to load up." Steven started to hand her a plate and then appeared to notice the bandage on her injured arm. "Never mind. I'll take care of it for you." Chicken and dumplings. Green beans that had been grown in the ranch garden. Sliced steamed carrots flavored with a hint of ginger.

Melanie followed Steven and her food to the dining room table. Once everyone was settled at the table with their food, they held hands and Jake spoke a blessing, thanking the Lord for the food, the opportunity for them all to be together, and for His love and protection. Then they dug in.

At first Melanie just moved her green beans around on her plate. She could appear fine in front of everyone, but she was still afraid, and her fear seemed determined to settle in her throat and stomach. But then she thought about the blessing Jake had just said. How sincere he sounded in saying something that people often said quickly and mostly through force of habit. Maybe his words seemed to carry more sincerity because of what he'd been through, losing his wife at such a young age.

She glanced at Alan and Kayla, who were eating and talking and dropping a fair amount of dumpling on the tablecloth each time they scooped up a spoonful of food.

Their dad was asking them about their day and what they did at school. How much pain must they have worked through after Janelle had passed away to reach this point, where they could function normally and actually enjoy life? In other conversations with Jake, he had made it clear to Melanie that faith played a huge role in getting him through his heartbreaking loss.

She took a deep breath, and when she blew it out, the fear that had lodged in her had loosened its hold a little. It was still there, but not nearly as strong. She was determined to focus on faith rather than fear.

And if she was going to recover from her injuries and get into fighting shape, she needed to eat. She took a bite of the chicken and dumplings. It was savory and delicious. She went for a second bite and glanced up. Luke caught her eye and nodded ever so slightly.

Yeah, I'm eating now, she thought. *But soon you and I are going to have a talk.* She wanted to know every detail of what he'd learned about the assailant. Pressing on in faith did not mean a person threw common sense out the window.

As soon as dinner was over, Luke mentioned to Jake that he needed to speak with him and Melanie. Tanya immediately offered to take the kids and Billy Clyde downstairs to watch a movie and pointedly looked at her husband, who, after an awkward few seconds of silence, grinned and declared that he would love to clean up the kitchen.

Melanie and Jake followed Luke into the front room, where he closed the blinds on all the windows, while Jake and Melanie each dropped down into a club chair.

Luke turned to Jake. "I wanted you to hear this because you should know of the potential danger you and the kids are in with Melanie here at the house."

Melanie shifted uneasily in her chair.

"Okay," Jake said, drawing out the word. "What's going on?"

Luke remained standing. "I'm not the only person at the sheriff's department working on Melanie's case. A couple of other deputies have been doing some research to help solve it. One in particular has been looking for any attacks with any similarity to what's been happening to Melanie. Eventually she made contact with a homicide detective in Kalispell, Montana, and a sheriff's deputy in Teton County, Wyoming, who had some important information to share."

Homicide detective. Melanie found her thoughts focused on those words and her heart thumped harder.

"Now that we've started to piece together some information, we'll be reaching out to other law enforcement agencies to see if there might be other victims."

"Victims of *what*?" Melanie blurted out. "What exactly have you pieced together?"

"One woman was shot to death in Wyoming. A woman was kidnapped and locked up in a storage shed, also in Wyoming.

Mercifully she survived. A third woman, in Montana, was injured by an improvised explosive device placed outside her home. After putting the information together, we realized all three women had something in common. They'd all worked at large public events. One had worked at a rodeo. One at a rock-and-mineral show. One at a county fair."

"Dwayne Skinner," Melanie muttered, shocked at the idea that the local rodeo hero could be the evil person behind all that had happened. "He must be the attacker. Those are all the sort of events he would attend."

Luke held up his hand. "We can't jump to conclusions. Getting tunnel vision during an investigation is never a good idea." He walked over and sat on the sofa near Melanie. "That said, Dwayne is the first person I thought of, too. But he didn't sponsor any of the events connected to the attacks. He didn't book any commercial flights or hotel rooms near the events. According to his flight records, he didn't fly his private plane to any of the events.

"It's important to remember that each of these events attracts a lot of cash sales, which are obviously a temptation to all sorts of unsavory people. Including career criminals like your employee Peter Altman's family."

Melanie stared toward the window even though it was impossible to see out of it. Her mind was spinning and her heart was breaking as she thought about what those other poor women had gone through.

She was also fighting back disappointment. She'd had high hopes that, while the news of a serial attacker was terrifying, it would at least give some focus to the investigation and narrow down their list of suspects.

She would be wary of Dwayne Skinner. Peter's family could somehow be involved, but she was convinced Peter was a decent guy.

Meanwhile Diana traveled the region,

looking for her own antique items to sell at The Mercantile. And there were plenty of other craftspeople and salespeople Melanie saw at various events around the northwest. She had to tell Diana and send out an email to the other members of her sales associations, letting them know that they could be in danger.

"Do you have any idea of a motive for the attacks?" Jake asked Luke. "Obviously you wouldn't have to go to those extremes just to rob somebody."

"The physical appearances of all three women are different, with the exception that all three are in the same age range. Twenty to thirty years old. So it doesn't look like he's targeting women based on appearance. My best guess right now is that all of the women witnessed something. Or at least the attacker thinks they did. It's possible that the women had some kind of interaction with the guy that set him off. Maybe a conversation that triggered some kind of rage in him. I don't know."

Melanie glanced over at Jake. His gaze was focused on the floor in front of him and he was worrying his bottom lip between his teeth. He had to be concerned for the safety of his children. If Melanie was thinking about that, most certainly it was on his mind, too.

"I appreciate you letting me stay here," Melanie said to him. He looked up at her. "But I'm looking forward to going home and sleeping in my own bed."

That was not exactly the truth. She would much rather stay here. But she had to put Kayla and Alan's safety ahead of her own.

"I think staying here a little longer might be wiser," Luke said.

She turned to him and saw the concern etched on his face. "I can't stay," she said. "Not when there's a chance that my being here could put the children in danger."

Jake turned to her. She could see both regret and gratitude in his eyes.

"The alarm system has been installed and tomorrow I'm going to go back to staying at Anna's house," Melanie said, trying to sound more confident than she felt.

"All right," Luke responded. "Then I'll be staying there, too."

NINE

"Tell me about your relationship with Dwayne Skinner." Miles County Sheriff Eric Chavez looked closely at Melanie and waited for her response. He wore wire-rimmed glasses, which Luke thought made him look like a college professor.

"Why don't we ask Mr. Skinner to expedite his return to town so we can question him?" Luke interjected. The events promoter was out of town and Luke was chomping at the bit to talk to him in person.

The sheriff shifted his attention to Luke and cocked an eyebrow. Luke gave him a slight nod in return. Yes, he knew he shouldn't have butted in. But for Melanie's sake he was getting impatient. Catching bad guys was his job and he loved doing it. On a personal level he didn't want Melanie to suffer through any more attacks, or have to push through any more fear. She was fighting hard to stay tough—he could see it—but he could also sense the strain it was taking on her.

The sheriff turned his attention back to Melanie. Luke did, too. He'd already asked her about Skinner. More than once. But in the sheriff's department building, with the sheriff in front of her and the power and authority of the department in full view, perhaps she'd say something different. Or add in something that she'd never mentioned before. The sheriff had instructed Luke to limit the information he shared with Melanie until the three of them met together, because he was interested in seeing Melanie's initial reactions.

"Do you think Dwayne is the person who's been attacking me?" Melanie asked. She rubbed her hand across the bandages on her opposite arm. She'd told Luke this morning, while they were eating breakfast before leaving the ranch, that the stitches were already starting to itch.

Shortly after that conversation Luke had gotten a call from the sheriff, asking him to bring Melanie by to talk with him before taking her back to Anna's house.

"I'm sure Lieutenant Baxter has already told you about the assaults on women in Wyoming and Montana, and how they have some elements similar to the attack on you. That changes things. The prior attacks on you were local news. Going forward, your story will likely become regional or even national news."

Melanie nodded that she understood.

"We need to be very careful about the information that gets into the news or that is dispersed on the internet." He took a deep breath. "All of this is a long-winded way of me telling you that Dwayne Skinner is not a suspect and I'm asking you not to characterize him as one in any conversations you have."

"I understand," Melanie said. "You have to look at the political side of things because that's part of your job. And you don't want anything to happen that might ruin the chances for a conviction once someone is charged. I will absolutely cooperate with you." She crossed her arms and tilted her head slightly, almost a mirror image of the way the sheriff was sitting. "Now, tell me, off the record, is Dwayne a suspect?"

Luke bit down on his lower lip to keep from grinning a little. The woman had backbone. He admired that.

"You first," the sheriff countered. "What's your relationship with him?"

Melanie uncrossed her arms. "There isn't much of one. When I moved back from California, I saw his TV ads and the billboards. I knew who he was. His promotions company was involved with some of the rodeos and different events I went to where I sold my jewelry and furniture. Diana eventually introduced us at The Mercantile."

"What did you and Skinner talk about?"

"Nothing significant." Melanie shrugged and glanced toward the window.

Luke followed her gaze and saw that it had started raining again.

"We'd talk about the weather," she continued, returning her gaze to the sheriff. "I talked to him when we bumped into each other at a few of the events he was promoting. He'd ask me how my business was doing. Maybe give me a little free advice on marketing and advertising, which I appreciated. He knows what he's doing in that area. But they always were short conversations. Mostly small talk. He approached me a couple of times offering to invest money in my business so I could expand it faster. I let him know I wasn't interested."

Melanie was telling the sheriff the same things she'd told Luke. He was disappointed that she hadn't added any new details.

"Now it's your turn," she said to the sheriff. "What are your thoughts about Dwayne Skinner?"

He leaned back in his chair. "We're looking at him closely right now for the obvious reasons. He has a private plane and we know he travels to events in Wyoming and Montana. And, of course, he knows you."

"Owning a private plane isn't exactly common in this part of the country, but it isn't unusual, either," Luke said. "There are at least a dozen ranches in this county alone with a plane on the property and room for a runway. Plus there are private planes kept at the regional airport."

"Is there some reason to assume an airplane was involved?" Melanie asked. "We're in the panhandle of Idaho, so Montana isn't that far away. Neither is Wyoming, really. I cross paths with plenty of other vendors at events who drive much farther distances than that to earn their living."

"There's no reason to assume a private

plane was involved," the sheriff said. "It's just one of the many elements we're taking a look at."

"I appreciate everything you're doing," Melanie said.

"Now that the investigation is expanding, we've asked the Bowen police for a little more help," the chief continued. "Specifically patrolling the neighborhood where you live and staging a patrol car downtown, in front of The Mercantile, if you're going back to working there."

Luke hoped Melanie would say she *wasn't* going back to work at the store. But she didn't. He wanted her tucked somewhere safely out of harm's way until this was over. Luke had already told the sheriff he'd offered to camp out on the couch in the living room at Anna's house when he was off duty, until the attacker was captured. Melanie needed someone there with the skills to protect her.

"I don't know if I'll be able to go back to

work at The Mercantile for the long-term," Melanie said to the sheriff. "But even if I stop working there, I'll have to go back at least once to wrap things up."

"Understood." The sheriff got to his feet, signaling that the meeting was over. He reassured Melanie that everything possible was being done to track down the perpetrator before he harmed her again or hurt anyone else.

Luke led Melanie through the break room before they left the building, grabbing them each a paper cup and filling it with freshly brewed coffee. The rain was still falling steadily outside. It would be good to have something to warm them up.

He wasn't especially eager to take her home. Yes, the new alarm system had been installed, but when he'd first recommended it, the attacker hadn't seemed so desperate. After the brazen attack at The Mercantile, Luke had changed his mind about that. The attacker apparently was desperate enough now to take extreme risks.

When they reached his truck he opened the passenger door for Melanie, then went around to the other side and climbed in. It was strange how comfortable he felt with her after knowing her just a short amount of time.

"What's the next step in your investigation?" Melanie asked after he'd started up the engine and turned on the heater.

He couldn't resist a slight smile as he turned to her. "Why do I suspect that you're asking because *you* have a plan?"

"I have no plan other than trying to stay alive." She reached up to tuck her hair behind her ear and Luke saw the bandage on her arm. If she weren't a fighter, that cut might have been across her throat instead of the arm she'd used to defend herself. And the cut might have been deeper. In which case everything would have been over for her.

"What are you thinking?" she asked.

He wondered what she saw expressed on his face. His admiration for her, maybe. His anger that someone had repeatedly assaulted her. His icy fear that he might not be able to stop the assailant in time.

"I'm just thinking it's a good thing you're scrappy," he said, trying to keep the mood from getting too dark.

She let go a small laugh. "If you make enough mistakes and don't give up on life, I guess your reward is that you end up scrappy."

Luke had been through some grim experiences in his life. And he supposed she was right. If you get knocked down and get back up enough times, you get pretty good at the getting back up part.

Her smile slowly faded and she looked closely at him again. It was a little unnerving having her attention focused on him like that. Other women had at one time or another directed their attention toward him. He'd had romantic relationships, though none had come close to marriage. Those other women in his life had looked *at* him. Melanie seemed to see things a little below the surface, as if she were looking *into* him. He wasn't so sure he liked that.

"Do you think it's possible to mess things up so spectacularly in your life that you ruin everything?" she asked. "I mean to the point that whatever good things God had planned for you are just off the table. You had your chance and you blew it?"

They were still in the parking lot. Luke was in no hurry to go anywhere. He considered her question. "Why do you ask?" he said. "What do you think you messed up so badly?"

She shrugged. "I guess I just feel like I made some bad choices in the past and wasted a lot of years. My marriage was a bad decision. Some of the things I did when I lived in California, before I came to my senses, were bad decisions." She sighed.

"Coming close to death makes you think about things like that."

"Yes, it does." Luke knew that very well. "I've made some choices in my life that weren't especially good. I don't know about specific events in your life, whether you can lose your chance at getting something you were meant to have. But I do believe walking in faith will give you the best life you can possibly have. And that's more important than getting the specific things you think you want."

She thought for a few seconds and then gave him a bright smile that made Luke feel like the dark clouds outside had parted, even though they had not. "Thank you."

Feeling emotionally exposed at the moment—a sensation Luke did not like at all—he quickly changed the subject. "I spent part of yesterday looking at the evidence left behind at the attack on you at The Mercantile. There wasn't much. The security system is limited to alarms on doors and windows, and cameras above cash registers placed to capture images of potential robbers. No image of the attacker was recorded, but the Bowen Police Department has an officer canvassing the neighborhood around the store to see if anyone saw anything."

"What's next?"

"I'd like to talk to Peter Altman again and follow up with his brothers. One of the other deputies finally caught up with them and questioned them, but they were pretty close-mouthed and he didn't get much useful information."

Melanie sighed. "I still don't think Peter is involved."

"I want to cover all the bases," Luke said. "And that means I want to talk to your ex-husband, too."

Melanie stared through the windshield, at the rain, which was now falling harder. Luke only saw her face in profile. He couldn't clearly read her expression, but he could see her shoulders slump. He would press for a little more information about her ex-husband later.

"How do you feel about going back to the fairgrounds for a quick look?" he asked. "The weather's too bad to get out and walk around again, but maybe since your memory is back you'll see something that will trigger a new memory of a useful detail."

"Okay," she said. "It's worth a try."

Luke put the truck into gear and they finally left the sheriff's department parking lot. It took just a few minutes to get to the fairgrounds. Melanie directed him to park where she had parked her own truck the evening of the attack. Then, in an unemotional, detached-sounding tone, she recounted aloud what she remembered about that night.

Sales were good for the three-day event. After she'd closed her sales booth and packed up everything, Peter had wanted to grab something to eat before they left. While he was gone, and Melanie was standing outside her truck, someone came up behind her in the deepening dusk and pressed a gun into the back of her neck.

There was the whispered threat. The forced walk toward the woods. The heart-pounding moment she realized that if she didn't get away, she was going to die in those woods. Sheer terror had energized her body into running as fast as she could. She'd raced between the trees, trying to shake off her attacker. She'd heard gunshots and then, the next thing she knew, she was opening her eyes and looking at the stars in the sky.

Luke listened closely for any new details, but he didn't hear any.

"Why is this happening to me?" she demanded, her voice sounding wobbly, as though she were choking back tears. "Why does this person want to torment me?"

Why me? was such a horrible, haunting question. Every time someone asked Luke that question, typically with pain-filled eyes, beseeching him for an answer, Luke said a quick prayer for that person. He did that now for Melanie. It was not the first time he'd prayed for her. Nor would it be the last.

"We might get an answer to that some-day," he said. *Or we might not get one in this lifetime.* He sighed. "It's frustrating, I know." He'd had his own dark moments, both as a soldier and a cop, when he'd asked why.

Luke scanned the parking lot as well as he could with so much rain pouring down. He wanted to make sure no one had followed them. He spotted Don Chastain's truck and made a mental note to call the chief of event security at the fairgrounds when he had a chance. There were people who helped pro-vide security as temporary employees at events all over the region. Don could direct him toward any one of those people whom he thought might be a viable suspect. That was a new angle to consider.

Luke turned to Melanie. "Are you ready to go?" Frankly he wasn't sure *he* was ready to go. Because he wanted to keep her close by his side. But having her with him while he questioned potential suspects was not a wise idea.

She wanted to go back to Anna's house rather than stay at the ranch, so he would take her there. Even with the new alarm system, and the Bowen Police Department keeping a close watch on the place, he wasn't sure he could leave her there and then drive away. But he had to. Because he had to stop the assailant before he attacked Melanie again.

It was nearing seven o'clock in the evening when Melanie got a text from Luke, telling her he was about to arrive at Anna's house.

It felt like it should be closer to midnight. Probably because summer had so swiftly and completely ended, which meant fall had arrived and the days were getting noticeably shorter. Or maybe it was because Melanie was just plain tired. Having to physically heal from the four attacks, and deal with the bewilderment and stress from having temporarily lost her short-term memory, as well as handling the cold, dark fear that came with all of it, was taking its toll on her.

"Luke is almost here," she said to Anna, who was sitting on the couch in the living room, after recently finishing a video chat with her husband.

"Good." Her cousin looked over at her. "The downstairs den is all his. I've already set out some sheets and blankets for him to put on the sofa bed. And a couple of pillows."

Anna seemed distracted and Melanie walked over to her. "If you don't want Luke to stay here—if you don't want *me* to stay here—just tell me. It's okay. I'd understand."

Anna tried to smile. "Really? Am I that bad of a host?"

Melanie sat down on the couch beside her. "You're a wonderful host. But I've become a pain of a guest. You had to have an alarm system installed because of me." At least the arrangements were in place for Melanie to take care of the bill. And a fairly substantial bill, it was.

"First of all you're not a guest. You're family," Anna said. "So of course you're a pain some of the time." She grinned, but then the grin slowly faded. She gestured toward the inactive electronic tablet beside her. "It's just that I had to tell Tyler about the security system and about Luke staying here."

"And he has a problem with that?" If so, Melanie was willing to change all of her plans and move out as soon as possible.

"No. He knows who Luke and his brother, Jake, are, though he doesn't exactly *know* them personally. They've got some mutual friends, including one who is also in the military, like Tyler, and knows Luke is a man of integrity."

Anna rubbed her eyes. "It's just that I can tell Tyler is getting really worried now that the guy attacking you might come to the house and I'll get hurt." She turned to Melanie and a blush reddened her cheeks. "He's worried about *me*." She rolled her eyes like she was embarrassed. "He's the one in a combat zone."

A feeling of regret, even for things she had no control over, gnawed at the pit of Melanie's stomach. Because of the attacks on her, and because she lived here, Anna was in danger.

"I'm just afraid Tyler is going to be so distracted by worrying about me that he's going to get hurt." Anna burst into tears. "I wasn't going to tell him everything, just so he wouldn't worry. But he stays in touch with some of the guys from church. I thought if he found out about things from them instead of me, it would make things even worse."

Melanie wrapped an arm around Anna's shoulder and gave her a squeeze. The pressures on someone who was left at home while a loved one was deployed were hard for anyone to imagine who hadn't been through it. Even living in the same house with Anna, it was easy to forget that her cousin was worried about Tyler all the time.

Maybe Melanie needed to move out. She already knew she needed to get back to work so she could pay for the alarm system. Not to mention to keep up with the rent she'd promised to pay Anna until Tyler came back home. But for the sake of Anna's safety and Tyler's peace of mind, maybe she needed to figure out an alternate living arrangement.

A tone sounded from a small speaker in the kitchen. Part of the security system to let them know somebody was coming up the walk. "That should be Luke," Melanie said. She tapped her phone to open the app showing the front of the house so she could be certain it was him.

It was indeed Luke. She unlocked the door and let him in. He had a duffel bag slung over one shoulder and a laptop in a case over the other. In his hands he carried a bag from a fast-food restaurant and a drink. It was still raining and he was soaked. When he saw Melanie, he gave her a weary smile and her heart leapt. Which was ridiculous, so she tried to coax it into settling down. This was not a social call. Her rebellious heart continued to flutter, anyway.

"Hey, how are you doing?" he asked.

She let a smile lift one corner of her mouth. "All things considered, I'm doing all right."

He exchanged greetings with Anna, who was still seated on the couch, as he set his things down in the foyer. He shrugged out of his dripping jacket and hung it on the coat tree, then picked up his bag of food and his drink. Melanie led the way to the kitchen.

"Are you sure you don't want some lasagna instead of whatever's in that bag?" she asked, gesturing toward the foil-covered casserole dish on the counter. "A couple of friends from church came over to keep me company today while Anna was at work. They brought the ingredients and we made the lasagna together."

"Thank you, but you don't need to feed me

while I stay here." He sat down at the small kitchen table, unwrapped a greasy burger, took a bite and then dumped a pile of fries on a thin paper napkin.

Melanie pulled out a chair and sat down with him. "Did you find out anything helpful about my case today?" she asked.

He shook his head and took a sip of his soda. "I talked to a lot of people. Got timelines from them, telling me where they were during the times you were attacked. I've got a lot of notes to look over and then piece together. It's a tedious and not-so-glamorous part of investigation, but at some point it usually pays off."

Anna wandered into the kitchen, letting Luke know the den was ready for him to use and encouraging him to make himself at home. She sat down and told him about her husband and their mutual friends.

Eventually Anna excused herself, saying she wanted to turn in early, and she went upstairs. Melanie showed Luke to the den, where he'd be staying. "I'm glad to see there's a desk," he said. "I'm going to go through my notes and organize them tonight."

"Okay." Melanie nodded and started to back out of the room, feeling disappointed that they weren't going to spend the evening together. Which was silly. He was here to work. Not to sit on the sofa and watch a movie with her.

"I need the contact information for your ex-husband," Luke said as he opened the case and removed his laptop.

"Investigating Ben will be a waste of your time," Melanie said. "There's no lingering animosity. He wanted the divorce. He made it excruciatingly clear that he didn't hate me. He was just bored with being married to me and simply wanted me to get out of the way so he could live a more exciting life." There was a stretch of time when that explanation would have come out sounding pained and bitter. Now it simply sounded kind of sad, but mostly factual. And that was how it felt.

Luke grabbed a pen and a scrap of paper. "Nevertheless I need his phone number and the numbers of anyone else in his family, if you've still got them."

Melanie had deleted those numbers from her phone a while ago, but she still knew Ben's number and his mother's by memory, so she rattled them off, with Luke jotting them down as she did.

She started to leave again so he could get to work. "Good night."

"Good night," Luke responded distractedly, his attention focused on the screen of his laptop as he got it powered up and running.

Just before she shut the door, he called out her name and she pushed it back open. "I'm sorry you were married to an idiot," he said. This time he had turned in the desk chair and was looking directly at her. "I hope you know whatever insulting garbage your former husband told you was a reflection on him and his character. It was not about you."

Melanie felt an ache in her heart. She should have married a man like this one.

"Thank you." Reluctantly she really left this time and closed the door behind her. The generous part of her nature hoped Lieutenant Luke Baxter found whatever excitement he was looking for when he eventually left town. The selfish part of her nature hated the thought that she'd have to live the rest of her life without ever seeing him again, once he was gone.

TEN

The alarm on Luke's phone went off early the next morning. It didn't matter that it was a Saturday. The reality of every job he'd ever had, from ranching to soldiering to policing, was that the job *had* to get done. Oftentimes getting caught up on sleep just had to wait.

He'd been up late, reading over his interview notes and creating more timelines based on each individual's reported activity during the time of the attacks on Melanie. He hadn't found a smoking gun yet, but when he verified each person's story, that could change.

He got ready for the day in the small bathroom across the hall from the den, where he'd slept, and then headed toward the kitchen, where the lights were on and the rich scent of coffee beckoned.

"I heard you moving around and figured you'd want some breakfast," Melanie said, turning from the stove to glance at him. She was dressed in overalls that were covered with multicolored paint splatters. The blue-checked flannel shirt she wore beneath it was rolled up at the sleeves. She'd pinned up her hair, but several strands had come loose and hung in wisps around her face.

She looked adorable and Luke couldn't stop staring at her. Fortunately she didn't seem to notice.

"I made a big pan of scrambled eggs with cheese. And fried potatoes." She pointed toward the coffeepot. A mug sat in front of it. "Help yourself," she said. "I like my coffee black, but there's cream in the fridge if you want it."

Luke liked his coffee black, too. And fortunately Melanie turned back around to finish cooking the potatoes before she realized Luke couldn't take his eyes off her.

He forced himself to turn his gaze away, poured some coffee and took a couple of sips. This moment with her, right now, felt comfortable and cozy. And also unsettling. Unsettling because he *liked* it.

Sure, he enjoyed being around the kids and Jake and their crazy dog. There were often moments, *family*-type moments at the ranch, which were pleasant. And admittedly he missed seeing Alan and Kayla this morning. But those warm moments had felt temporary. Even though the ranch had been his childhood home, he sometimes felt like a guest there. He'd always assumed Jake would get married again, someday. Then Jake, his new wife and the kids would be a family unit, and Luke would be outside of that. On his own. Moving on. Looking for the next adventure, because that's how he liked to live his life.

Comforting domestic moments made him

nervous. Because he knew they wouldn't last. After his mom had died and his dad had become emotionally withdrawn, Luke had learned that chasing an adrenaline rush, whether it was in a kayak, swirling atop the rapids on a raging Idaho river, or racing down a double black-diamond run on a Rocky Mountain ski slope, helped fill the sense of emptiness in his life. Faith filled his life with meaning. But danger and excitement chased away the sense of missing something in his day-to-day existence.

So, what exactly was happening right here and now in this kitchen with Melanie?

He didn't know.

With her back still to him, Melanie reached for plates in the cabinet and dished up the food.

"Is Anna joining us?" Luke asked, taking a plate of food and walking beside Melanie to the dining room table, where they each took a seat.

"I don't know." Melanie sat down and took

a noisy slurp of her coffee. "I haven't seen her yet."

"You're up early," Luke said before taking a bite of the fried potatoes. They had bits of onion and green pepper, and they were delicious. "Were you having trouble sleeping?" Post-traumatic stress was real, and he couldn't help worrying about her.

Melanie sighed. "Yes. I had a lot on my mind. Most of my inventory in the storage space got ruined in the explosion. All of the furniture I'd bought to restore was a total loss."

She paused to eat a bite of the scrambled eggs. "Fortunately I had a few pieces of furniture stored in the shed here. So I brought them onto the sunporch to get started on cleaning them."

"You don't worry about harming their value when you do that?"

"You watch antique shows on TV, don't you?" She smiled at him and he wanted to kiss her. But that wasn't going to happen.

Not while he was a cop whose job it was to protect her. "The pieces I'm working on right now aren't really antiques," she continued, oblivious to his impulse to turn their relationship into something that was completely inappropriate at the moment. "So worrying about cleaning decreasing their value isn't an issue."

There was the sound of footsteps on the stairs, and a few seconds later Anna popped into the dining area, dressed for the day and looking full of energy. "Ah, I didn't just dream that I smelled coffee and fried potatoes." She headed for the kitchen, calling out "Good morning" as an afterthought. She quickly reappeared, carrying her breakfast and a mug of coffee, and she and Melanie chatted while all three of them ate.

Luke needed to go to work. There were people he wanted to talk to in person, plus phone calls to other law enforcement agencies he wanted to make. After excusing himself, he took his plate and mug to the kitchen and put them in the dishwasher. The sun was coming up, and looking out the kitchen window above the sink, he saw a Bowen Police Department patrol car parked at the curb. He knew city police couldn't keep an officer out there all of the time—their staff was too small for that—but any show of presence was helpful as a deterrent to keep the attacker away. At least he hoped so.

He went back to the dining room to say goodbye to the ladies and was surprised to walk into a somewhat emotional conversation. The gist seemed to be that Anna had declined an invitation to attend some sort of social event later this afternoon so she could stay at the house with Melanie.

"Go to the baby shower," Melanie was insisting. "I'm sure Luke won't be too late coming back to the house." She glanced in his direction. "Or I could call a friend to come over."

Anna looked doubtful.

"What time does the party start?" Luke asked Anna.

"Four o'clock."

"I'll make sure I'm back by then." He turned to Melanie. "Maybe we can ride out to the ranch if you want to. The kids won't be there. They're staying with Janelle's parents tonight." He had his sheriff's department pickup truck, since he was on call over the weekend. It seemed very unlikely the assailant would try to harm Melanie while she was riding with him. "Jake usually fires up the barbeque on Saturday nights," he continued. "I'll tell him to make sure he has a couple of extra steaks for us."

The anxious expression on Melanie's face eased into a smile. She reached up to tuck some of the wisps of hair around her face back behind her ears, fussing with them like she'd just noticed they were there. Her cheeks flushed a little. "Sounds like a great idea."

"I got married right out of high school," Melanie said to Tanya. "And my new husband wanted to move to California right away. Anything sounded more exciting than staying here in Bowen, Idaho.

"I hadn't had any kind of job training, but it turned out I was a natural-born saleswoman," she added. Which was a good thing. The beaches and the sunny weather were warm and welcoming. The cost of living down there, however, was a cold shock. "I love antiques and vintage items," Melanie continued. "And I'd made silver jewelry for myself and my friends ever since I took a jewelry-making class in high school. When my marriage fell apart I knew I wanted to move back home, and I knew I wanted to start my own business combining several things that I loved to do."

She and Tanya sat across from each other on matching comfortable, plump sofas in the downstairs great room in the Baxter family ranch house. Dinner had been delicious. Melanie could see Luke, Jake and Steven on the patio, on the other side of the glass slider. They were doing a little cleanup, but mostly they were standing around, talking. The scruffy-looking dog, Billy Clyde, was quietly lying on the floor, looking like he missed the kids.

"I know from experience it can be exhausting running your own business," Tanya said. She took a sip from her mug of decaf. "I imagine you'll have to close up shop until the attacks on you are finally stopped."

The slider opened and the guys walked in, carrying the cooking utensils from the barbeque.

"I can't close down my business completely," Melanie said in answer to Tanya's comment. "I've already had customers calling me with complaints." She glanced toward Luke and caught his eye. While the other two men headed upstairs to the kitchen, he lingered behind, listening.

"People *complained*?" Tanya said, sounding indignant.

"To be fair, one was the owner of a gift shop down in Coeur d'Alene. She hadn't heard about the attacks on me. The other person who complained is a lady in town who's been waiting for me to finish restoring a vanity she brought to me. Fortunately I had it at Anna's house so it didn't get damaged. She has company coming next weekend and she wants it installed before they arrive. She also bought a mirror from me and I need to get that to her. I told her I'd take care of it on Monday."

"I can handle it," Luke interjected. He was standing behind the sofa, where Melanie was seated, and she'd turned so she could glance between him and Tanya.

"I'd really appreciate your help," she said to him. "Thank you." Had she thanked him before now? Probably not enough. But he had to know how much she appreciated all he was doing for her. "I know my life is more important than my business," she added. "But I don't want to lose everything I've worked for, if I can help it."

"What about opening an online store?" Tanya asked.

"I will definitely be setting up an online store. I'd meant to do it eventually, anyway. I've already ordered supplies to make more jewelry. I figure that will be easy to ship to customers. I haven't decided yet what to do with the few small pieces of furniture I have left and the items that are still at The Mercantile."

Jake walked halfway down the staircase and called to his dog to come upstairs if he wanted his dinner. Like Billy Clyde, Jake seemed a little bit lost without his kids around, even though, unlike his dog, he obviously knew they were only going to be gone one night.

Melanie glanced over at Luke, who was also watching his brother. For the moment he'd let down his guard, set aside the tough-guy demeanor. There was an almost boyish expression on his face. She thought it looked like gratitude. As if he were delighted to see his brother looking happy.

From the moment her ex-husband had told her he was filing for divorce, Melanie had been convinced that the path of her life would forever be something different than what she'd wanted. No children. No family of her own. She was afraid that everything had gotten out of step and would stay that way. But here was proof that people healed. New paths opened up. God was certainly not surprised by the turn of events, and He could offer a new plan and purpose for a life that had taken an unexpected and disappointing turn.

"Hey, slacker!" Jake called over to Luke a few seconds later. "Quit hiding out with the ladies just so you can avoid washing dishes." Jake had insisted that the guys could take care of clean-up.

Luke grinned at him. "You're just jealous because you didn't think of it first." He headed up the stairs.

Melanie watched him go, and then exchanged smiles with Tanya.

The feeling of nervous tension that had settled in the pit of her stomach, and stayed there ever since the attack at the fairgrounds, was still there. As were the various aches and pains she still suffered as a result of the attacks. But for the moment she was going to let herself enjoy the sense of security she felt with this family, which was made up of people who were all complete strangers to her less than two weeks ago. It was amazing how that had all come together.

An hour later she was back in the truck with Luke and heading for Anna's house. The heater was on, but it was still hard to shake the chill she'd caught walking from the ranch house to the truck in the drizzling rain.

"I talked to Jake about delivering that vanity and mirror you mentioned," Luke said as they pulled out from the ranch's driveway, onto the road. "Just get me the address and any other information I'll need, and we'll take care of it."

"Okay, I will." She was grateful for the help. At the same time, it made her a little nervous. Despite her determination to depend only on herself for the rest of her life after her divorce, she was getting used to having Luke help her with practical things, and she was leaning on him for emotional support. That was a little scary. How was she going to feel once her case was solved and Luke moved on? Or, if her case wasn't solved fairly quickly, what would she do if the sheriff's department reassigned Luke and had some other deputy take over her case? No matter how dedicated that person was, things wouldn't be the same.

As they headed down the road, Luke shifted his attention back and forth between the road ahead and the rearview mirror. She knew he was watching to see if they were being followed.

"I talked to Dwayne Skinner out at the airport today," Luke said after they'd ridden in silence for a few minutes.

"What did you learn?" Melanie asked, worried that this was the start of some bad news. "And why are you just telling me now? Why didn't you tell me earlier?"

"On the ride out here, you seemed to want to talk about everything other than your case. I figured you needed a break from thinking about it."

That was true. She had chattered about all kinds of things. Because, just for a while, she'd wanted to feel like a normal person again. Fearing for her life was exhausting. Even though she'd mostly been able to sleep at night, she never felt like she'd really caught up on her rest. Not since the attacks had started.

"His flight records confirmed what he'd already told us. That he didn't fly to any of the events in Wyoming or Montana near where the other women were attacked. He told me he was at his home, just outside of town, the night you were attacked at the fairgrounds. And he mentioned without my asking that he was at The Mercantile shortly before you were attacked there."

"So, where does that leave us with the investigation?" Melanie asked. "Is he in the clear?"

"Nobody is in the clear right now," Luke said. "But Dwayne was cooperative and he doesn't seem to have a motive. I'm still trying to interview Peter Altman's brothers for a second time. Both have criminal records and could be looking at lengthy prison sentences if they were caught with stolen goods again. So if they think you saw them with stolen goods, or doing something else illegal, it could make them desperate."

Melanie shook her head. "I don't remember seeing anything like that."

"Also I've left a couple of phone messages for your ex-husband, but he hasn't called me back. I spoke briefly to his mother, but she wasn't too anxious to talk to me, so I didn't learn much from her."

"Well, he always was a bit of a mama's boy." Melanie looked at her own side mirrors. She could see headlights from a vehicle roughly a mile behind them. Was that a threat? Or was it just someone out for a drive? And how could she possibly tell the difference until someone actually tried to kill her again?

They passed through an unmarked crossroads, and Luke slowed slightly to watch for cross traffic before moving on. Melanie watched to see if the car behind them sped up to catch up with them, but it didn't.

"After talking to several people today, I did learn something that concerns me," Luke said.

Great. Because she needed to hear about something *concerning* right now. She glanced over at him and saw him check his rearview mirror a couple of times. Apparently keeping an eye on the vehicle behind them.

"Word got out about your amnesia," he continued, his voice calm despite the tense set of his jaw. "But people don't know that you've recovered your memory."

"Okay. Why is that especially concerning?"

She glanced back at the mirror and saw that the headlights that had been behind them were gone. Perhaps the driver had turned at the crossroads.

"It's possible that whoever is trying to kill you knows about the amnesia and will want to finish the job before you recover your memory. Maybe they're afraid that recovering your memory will help you identify them."

"But that's not the case. I remember those two weeks I'd lost, and I still have no idea who is after me or why."

"But the assailant doesn't know that. Which would motivate him to attack you again, soon. Before you could report his identity to the police."

Melanie's fear spiked. She crossed her arms over her chest and pulled them close to her body. It was ridiculous to think she could physically hold herself together when she was on the verge of falling to pieces. But at the moment she didn't feel like she had a lot of other options.

ELEVEN

"I'm happy the mirror wasn't damaged during the attack on me," Melanie said to Diana. "It was already sold, but I'd left it here until I had a chance to deliver it."

Diana sighed. "I'm happy you didn't sustain any life-threatening injuries in that attack." She shook her head. "And I'm so sorry it happened in my store."

They were in The Mercantile, in the area where Melanie's jewelry and furniture were located. Jake was about to carry a full-length mirror in a pecan frame out to his truck and secure it in the back, alongside the vanity Melanie had made from a restored dresser. Luke stood near Melanie, with his hands empty so he could reach for the gun he had holstered under his loosely fitted shirt, if he needed it. He was not in uniform. This trip to help Melanie was being taken on his own time.

He took a step closer to her, trying to signal his impatience. Police in Wyoming had discovered another murder that might be attributable to the person who'd attacked Melanie. Meanwhile the surviving victim in the case couldn't give much useful information about the attacker. She'd been blindsided and couldn't say for certain if the assailant was a man or a woman. For that matter she'd been knocked unconscious, so they couldn't confirm that the attack had been carried out by a single individual. There could have been multiple attackers.

Luke blew out an impatient puff of air. He knew it was rude, but he wasn't playing around. He wanted to get Melanie out of here, get the furniture delivered to her customer and get her home. His original plan was that he and Jake would deliver the items without her coming along. But at the last minute she'd decided she wanted to accompany them so she could talk to the customer in person and apologize for the delay in delivery.

Melanie had a doctor's appointment tomorrow, and after that she'd agreed to stay at the house as much as possible until the attacker was captured.

She glanced at him, nodded slightly and then returned to her conversation with Diana.

Keeping her business afloat was not worth risking her life. But Luke also knew she needed something to look forward to. Otherwise she might become disheartened in the days ahead, when she would be locked up in Anna's house, almost as if she were the criminal.

She needed to keep her business going because it gave her a sense of power and control in her life. And that was important after being the victim of four violent attacks.

When he'd initially returned from combat, Luke had gone for a few sessions of therapy. It was hard to reject his dad's theory that real men didn't "carry on" about their feelings, but he'd done it. The nightmares had been too exhausting, and depression was not something to toy with. It was good to be able to draw on some of the things he'd learned while helping Melanie.

Still, she needed to wind up her conversation. "You can call Diana later," he finally said. "Let's go." And she ignored him again.

Melanie was her own woman. That was evident. From her behavior after the attacks, to her determination to keep her financial commitments to her cousin and keep her business afloat, she knew what her priorities were. And from what he could see, she'd done an amazing job of restructuring her life after going through a divorce she had not wanted. The more time he spent around her, the more he admired her.

He wondered if Melanie would ever consider getting married again.

He'd turned that question over in his mind several times since yesterday, when he'd accompanied her to church again. He'd stood at the back of the sanctuary, where he'd had a good view of all the entrances, so he could thwart any potential attack. And, of course, he'd kept an eye on Melanie.

She'd chosen to sit in the back pew, close to where he was standing. The sermon focused on God's faithful and steadfast love, and Luke had thought about what that meant. And about the qualities of faithfulness and steadfastness in a person.

Later, after the sermon was over and Melanie was taking a few minutes to chat with some friends, Luke had found himself glancing around the sanctuary and thinking about weddings. He'd been to a few, but only because he would have felt like a jerk if he hadn't gone. And he'd been the best man at his brother's wedding, which had turned out to be surprisingly fun.

Now here he was with Melanie, helping her deliver some furniture to one of her customers while he kept an eye out for the bad guy, or bad *guys*, who wanted to hurt her. He was vigilant at the moment and admittedly impatient to get her out of the store, but he didn't have that overall edgy, restless feeling he was used to. The one that he typically eased by doing something that got his adrenaline pumping. Or better yet kept completely at bay by diving so deeply into soldiering or policing or just about anything so all-consuming that it took his mind off how he felt.

So with that familiar, edgy, restless feeling gone, how did he feel now? Especially when he was around Melanie? Calm. And a little afraid that this feeling of calmness would go away when this case was solved and she no longer needed him.

"Can I talk to Peter for a minute?" Luke

heard Melanie ask Diana. He turned his attention toward their conversation.

"Peter took off for lunch just before you got here," Diana said.

"Was that his scheduled lunch break?" Luke asked. He still didn't quite trust Peter.

"It's a little bit early for his break," Diana said with a shrug. "But we were slow and he asked if he could go."

"Did he know Melanie and I were on our way here?" Luke was thinking not just about Peter, but also about his criminal brothers. They'd finally made themselves available to answer questions but hadn't offered any information that helped the investigation. Luke was still in the process of verifying their alibis for all of the attacks. In the meantime they'd dropped out of sight again. Their father claimed they'd gone on an extended fishing trip in an area where there was no phone service. When Luke had asked for an exact location, the father had not been able to give him one.

"I didn't specifically tell Peter you were coming," Diana said.

"Could he have overheard your conversation with Melanie when she called to tell you we were on our way here?"

"I suppose so."

Had Peter learned where Melanie was going to be within the next hour? Had he gotten the customer's address and would he tell the assailant, whether that was one of his brothers or some other criminal connected to the shadowy family business, where Melanie was going to be so they could try again to kill her?

"We need to leave *now*," Luke said to Melanie.

She nodded. "All right."

When they got to the truck, Luke would discuss a possible change in plans with her. Maybe it would be wiser if Melanie and Luke went back to Anna's house and stayed there. Jake could deliver the furniture on his own. There was a wheeled dolly from the ranch in the back of the truck. He could handle it.

Melanie, Luke and Jake walked toward the front door. Diana walked with them.

"I'm afraid I have to move my entire business out of The Mercantile," Melanie said to Diana as they walked side by side. "Right now I think it's smarter and safer to do everything online."

"Why don't you let me buy your inventory and resell it?" Diana asked.

"Maybe I could sell you a few items. But I'll need something to sell to get the online business started," Melanie answered. "I've ordered some supplies to make jewelry so I can stay busy while I'm stuck in the house." She gave Diana a weary smile. "It could be a long time before it's safe for me to get out and scout for old furniture in need of repair again."

Diana shook her head. "I'm sorry to see you go."

"Thank you," Melanie said. "I'll come

back in a day or so to get the rest of my stuff out of here and we'll talk about what you might want to buy."

Finally they walked out the door.

Jake walked ahead, carrying the mirror, while Luke stayed close to Melanie and scanned the area around them as they followed him. Nothing appeared out of the ordinary, but he was taking nothing for granted. He kept his right hand near his gun, just in case he needed it.

Peter leaving early today troubled Luke. Maybe the kid knew something. Maybe he felt guilty and wanted to avoid Melanie. Maybe he was afraid of being questioned again by Luke.

There was something else that also troubled him. Word would quickly get out that Melanie had closed shop at The Mercantile and would start working exclusively from home. That information might prompt the assailant to launch another attack on her as quickly as possible. To try to kill her before she was out of reach.

"The cut on your arm is healing nicely," Dr. Martin said, stepping back from Melanie to lean against a counter in the examining room. "Nevertheless all of the stress you're under isn't helping your overall health. I'm glad your memory is back, but you're still in recovery mode. You need to take it easy. You've been through a lot."

"But I'm bouncing back," Melanie said, sitting on the examining table, forcing a smile.

The doctor nodded, then looked pointedly at Melanie's hands. Melanie looked down to see her fingers interlaced so tightly that her knuckles were white.

Okay, maybe she wasn't exactly *bouncing back*. In truth she was tense every morning when she woke up and every night when she went to sleep. Luke kept her up-to-date on the investigation. It seemed like every day confirmed the possibility that any of the known suspects could be the assailant, without ever narrowing it down to any specific one.

It felt like they were getting nowhere. She'd seen news stories of women who were tormented by deranged stalkers for *years*. Was that how she would spend the rest of her life, in fear, hiding out in Anna's house?

"It's exhausting to have someone trying to kill you," Melanie said. Hearing those words come out of her mouth didn't seem real. And yet it was. The fear. The uncertainty. The lonely, hollow feeling of helplessness. They were all real.

"It's not unusual to feel like you're experiencing traumatic events anew, even after they've passed," the doctor said, as if reading Melanie's mind. "Sometimes it helps to talk about it."

Sometimes Melanie did talk to Anna and her friends and even Luke about what she was going through. But it felt as if she was complaining to the very people who were already doing so much for her.

"The thing that would help the most would be for the cops to catch the guy and lock him up," Melanie said.

The doctor nodded. "I understand that. And I'd like to see you in another two weeks."

Tanya was in the waiting room, flipping through a magazine, when Melanie exited the business area of the doctor's office.

"Did the doctor give you good news?" Tanya asked, standing up and tossing the magazine onto a table.

"I'm fine. Thanks for coming with me." Tanya and Steven were both welders and owned their own business. Tanya was able to take time away from their shop this morning without taking a hit in the wallet. Asking Anna to take time off work and come with her to the appointment was the last thing Melanie wanted to do after everything else she was putting her cousin through. And while Luke was assigned to her case, she couldn't keep dragging him away from his duties to be her personal bodyguard.

"So, that magazine I was looking at had some really cool old wooden doors that had been repurposed into jewelry boxes and storage cabinets," Tanya said as they stepped outside the doctor's office, into the hallway of the medical building. "Have you ever thought of doing something like that?"

Melanie barely registered the question. Moving from the interior of a building where she felt relatively safe to an area like an outside hallway was a nerve-racking ordeal for her. Her stomach felt like it was going to climb up into her throat as she quickly looked to her left and right. Just to make sure no one was there waiting for her. An attack could come from any direction, at any moment.

Tanya was also looking around. Melanie saw her slip her hand under the flap of her purse, where she kept a pistol, and she held it there. Tanya had been raised in the wilderness of North Idaho and knew how to shoot.

Tension made the surface of Melanie's skin feel tighter as they headed toward a wide staircase. They were on the third floor of the medical building. On arrival they'd made the decision not to use the elevator so they wouldn't have to worry about getting trapped inside it with a stranger. A concern that seemed to Melanie both outrageously dramatic and completely reasonable at the same time.

Sometimes she felt like she'd forgotten what normal life was like.

"I've seen some interesting things made from old doors," Melanie said, answering Tanya's earlier question. She didn't want to be rude to someone helping her, just because she felt anxious. They made it down to the first floor without incident and Melanie was starting to feel a little silly for being so nervous. The building was full of busy medical practices. There were plenty of people around, especially here in the main-floor lobby.

Outside, a brisk breeze ruffled her hair and rushed over her cheeks, chilling her skin. It wasn't far to Tanya's truck. Soon she would be home where she would feel safer.

"Melanie!"

She knew the voice, but she didn't turn to look at the person calling out to her. Instead she dropped her head a little and moved faster.

"Who is that?" Tanya asked, looking around.

Melanie could hear the footfalls of someone jogging up behind them. The skin began to crawl up the back of her neck. This was a man she *knew* she could not trust, and she wanted nothing to do with him. But she could hear him getting closer. She slowed her pace and looked at Tanya. "It's Ben. My former husband."

They both stopped walking and turned to face him. "Do we need to call the police?" Tanya asked.

Did they? Melanie didn't know. As Ben drew closer she thought about what a stranger he was to her now. Could he mean her harm? And as far as she knew, he still lived in California. So, what was he doing here?

In fact Luke had told her just last night that he'd spoken with Ben's parents again. They'd assured him that, while Ben had recently been in town for a short visit, he'd gone back to California a couple of days ago.

"I thought that was you," Ben said when he reached them.

There was an awkward beat of silence while Melanie waited for him to tell her why he was chasing her. It had been more than a year since she'd talked to him in person, but he'd called her a couple of times since then, asking her how she'd been able to afford to start her own business. He'd accused her of hiding financial assets from the court while their divorce was being processed. She'd assured him that that was not the case.

"Are you out for a leisurely lunch?" he finally asked.

That was an odd question.

He glanced at Tanya. All things considered, Melanie didn't feel compelled to make the introductions between the two of them. "Business must be good if you can afford to have lunch with a friend and go shopping in the middle of the day," he added. The medical building they'd just left was located in a section of town with several restaurants and quaint shops nearby. Before she and Ben had moved to California, Melanie had often come down here with a friend or two to shop, eat and unwind.

For possibly the millionth time Melanie wondered if Ben had changed after they moved to California, or if those deep character flaws had already been there but she'd been blind to them.

Either way she wanted nothing to do with him now. And the sense of situational awareness she'd developed over the last couple of weeks told her that standing here in this open parking lot was a bad idea.

"Take care," she said. Then she turned and resumed walking toward Tanya's truck.

Ben hurried past her and then stopped in front of her, blocking her path.

Tanya caught up to Melanie. "We need to get going," she said. She pulled her phone out of her back pocket.

Ben rolled his eyes and crossed his arms over his chest. Then he focused his gaze on Melanie. There was such malevolence in his eyes that it triggered a ripple of gooseflesh across the surface of her skin. There had been a time when she had known this man. At least she *thought* she had. But now he was a stranger to her. And she wasn't sure what he was capable of.

"If you cheated me out of a share of money that was rightfully mine, I am going to get it. You can count on that. We deserve a good start."

"We?"

The malevolent glare turned into a smirk. "I'm getting married. This time to the right woman."

"Let's go," Tanya said firmly. She took a couple of steps, then gestured at Melanie to follow her.

For a few seconds Melanie couldn't move, stunned as the possibility crossed her mind that Ben really could have something to do with the attacks on her. She had been fairly certain that if he was the one who had pressed a gun into the back of her neck and whispered a threat, she would have recognized his voice. But maybe not. Or maybe he'd hired someone.

She'd thought the idea of Ben being behind the attacks absurd, but now it did seem possible. Which meant she needed to get away from him *now*. She caught up with Tanya and they hurried to the truck. After Melanie got inside, she realized her whole body was trembling. Tanya fired up the engine and backed out of the parking slot. As she shifted gears and the truck started to move forward, Melanie glanced over her shoulder. Her ex-husband was still standing there in the parking lot. And his smirk had turned back into a glare.

"Your ex-husband has proven himself a jerk several times over," Anna said. Melanie had waited until Anna had come home from work that evening to tell her what had happened. "But do you really think he'd physically harm you? And for what reason?"

"I know it doesn't make any sense," Melanie said glumly. "But hardly anything does anymore." She was sitting on a stool in the kitchen, sipping tea while her cousin finished chopping the fresh tomato, onion and cilantro toppings for the pot of chili she'd started in a slow cooker before she'd left for work earlier in the day. Corn bread muffins were still cooling in a muffin tin on the countertop beside the oven. Anna liked to unwind by cooking and had declined Melanie's offer of help.

"Ben is convinced I hid money from him during the divorce." Melanie shook her head. "But harming me wouldn't benefit him financially." She stopped and thought for a minute. "Or would it? I don't have an actual will. As my former husband, if something happened to me, could he claim a right to inheritance?" Not that there would be much to inherit.

"I don't think so," Anna said. "But maybe you should talk to a lawyer and find out."

Tanya had insisted Melanie call Luke after their encounter with Ben and tell him what had happened. Luke had met them at Anna's house, listened to Melanie's recounting of the events with a stony expression on his face and then left after getting Tanya's promise that she'd stay with Melanie until Anna came home.

Tanya had sat in the living room where she could keep an eye on Melanie, and she seemed happy to talk anytime Melanie wanted to strike up a conversation. Otherwise, she stayed busy on her laptop working on various reports and spreadsheets related to her family's welding business.

Despite having Tanya there for company, the afternoon had dragged by.

Maybe Ben was a threat to her. Maybe he was the least of her worries. If she thought about it for very long, the world seemed like a horribly dangerous place. She felt certain there would be another attack. Anticipating it was like watching a violent storm slowly approaching. There wasn't much she could do to prepare for it. Mainly just hunker down and pray.

Melanie's phone chimed, startling her slightly. It was a text from Luke, letting her know that he would be driving up to the house in just a minute. She walked out to the front room. There was a splash of light discernible around the edges of the drawn shades. She tapped the security-monitor app on her phone and recognized Luke's truck.

"Well, we made it through another day," she said when he walked into the house, forcing a smile.

He gave her a slight smile in return, but it didn't reach his eyes. What she really wanted was for him to wrap his arms around her and hold her close. Give her a few moments when she felt completely protected. Let her feel the strong, steady beat of his heart.

Just seeing Luke made her feel safer. Not only because of his size, or because he was a lawman, but because she'd seen and heard enough from people who really knew him to believe he truly was as he presented himself to be. Trustworthy. A man of faith.

Despite the warnings she'd been whispering to herself for days to guard her heart, she was falling for him. She couldn't deny it anymore—not to herself. But he was a kind, considerate man who deserved the chance to live the life he wanted. And he'd made it clear he wanted a life of excitement and danger and travel. While Melanie's heart craved a family, stability and peace.

"Dinner's ready," Anna called out from the kitchen.

After making sure the front door was locked behind him, Luke took off his uniform jacket, hung it on the coat tree in the hall and went to wash up. A few minutes later the three of them were saying grace at the table and then digging in. Melanie was not especially hungry, but she knew she needed to eat.

"Did you learn anything about Ben?" she asked after eating a spoonful of chili.

Luke nodded. "I confirmed with his parents that they honestly thought after a quick visit he'd gone back home to California. That's what he'd told them. And they explained that they hadn't talked extensively to me before because they thought you were just drumming up some phony accusations to get him into trouble because you were still angry that he'd divorced you.

"Once I made it *abundantly* clear that you were in serious danger and their son had been acting in a threatening manner, they changed their tune. They think he's innocent of any wrongdoing, so they want to do whatever they can to clear him as a suspect. They told me he'd driven up here, rather than flying, so on a hunch I put out a 'be on the lookout' for his car. It was spotted in the parking lot of the Golden Gem Motel, out by the Interstate."

"Did you talk to him?" Melanie asked.

Luke nodded. "He said he'd brought his fiancée with him to Bowen. He wanted to show her his hometown. He knew his parents wouldn't allow the two of them to stay together at their house, and his fiancée said she wouldn't even consider staying in separate rooms, so he figured it would be easier to keep her hidden at the hotel and introduce her to his parents at a later time.

"He told me he got tired of staying at his parents' home by himself, but he still had a few more things he wanted to do in town and a few more people to visit. So he lied to them, told them he was going home to California, and then went to stay at the hotel with his fiancée, instead."

"Did you ask him if he'd attacked me?" Melanie asked.

"He said he had not. That he has no reason to hurt you. He claims he just happened to see you and got a little overzealous trying to talk to you."

"And you believe him?" she asked hopefully. Because it would be a horrible thing to know that her ex-husband had tried to kill her.

"What I *believe* is that he clearly understands you don't want him anywhere near you. I made certain of that. And he knows if you see him again, you will call 9-1-1 immediately."

Luke seemed to be waiting for confirmation, so Melanie nodded. "Okay."

"And trust me, we'll be taking a close look

at your former husband. His whereabouts for the last six months, where he's used his credit cards, firearms purchases—everything we can think of. After ambushing you today, he's moved to the top of my suspect list."

The newly installed motion-triggered light outside the kitchen door came on. Luke was on his feet in an instant and headed in that direction. Melanie quickly checked the security-monitor app on her phone.

From the screen on her phone, she could see the step outside the door was empty except for Luke. She nervously watched him disappear into the darkness as he went to search the property. She followed his progress, as much as possible, on the various camera feeds. Finally he returned through the kitchen door.

"Did you see anyone?" Melanie asked.

Luke shook his head. "No. I didn't see anybody."

"The neighbors have cats," Anna said

nervously. "Maybe one of them triggered the light."

"Maybe," Luke said.

Melanie didn't think he sounded convinced.

TWELVE

"I thought it would take longer than this to get my things packed up," Melanie said to the part-time cashier, Ginny, at The Mercantile. Not that Melanie wanted to spend the rest of the evening at the store, taking down her displays and packing everything up, but it was disheartening to see how little she would have available to sell at her new online store.

Ginny smiled sympathetically.

The two women were in Diana's office, toward the back of the store. Peter was seated in a chair in the corner. Melanie was signing the final paperwork that would officially end her connection with The Mercantile. She was also picking up the check Diana had left for her, covering payment for a few of Melanie's items that had sold during the last week. Melanie had phoned Diana as she left the house to let her know she was on her way, but the call had gone to voice mail.

Officer Sheila Burns of the Bowen Police Department stood in the doorway, alternately glancing into the office and then toward the front of the store. At Luke's request the police department had agreed to stage an officer downtown while Melanie was wrapping up things at The Mercantile. A couple of hours earlier Luke had followed Melanie to the store, in his sheriff's department truck, while she drove his pickup. Shortly after they had arrived, Officer Burns had walked into the store and introduced herself. She'd stayed within view of Melanie ever since.

"Any chance Diana will be back soon?" Melanie asked after she finished with the paperwork. When she arrived she'd been disappointed to learn Diana wasn't there.

"She didn't tell me where she was going," Ginny said. "But I assume she'll be back before we close."

"I can call her later. I just wanted to tell her my timeline for getting my bookcases and display cases out of here."

"I can help you move those if you want to do it now," Peter offered.

He'd helped her earlier as she'd packed things up and put them in the back seat of Luke's truck.

Peter had been polite, but not as friendly as he was back before the attacks had started. Luke had questioned him several times since he'd showed up at Anna's house, confessing his connection to his criminal family. It must be obvious that Luke still considered him a possible suspect. As were his brothers, who were clearly going out of their way to avoid further interviews with the authorities.

"Thank you," she said to Peter in response to his offer of help. "But I don't have space cleared out for them in the shed at Anna's yet."

"I think this is Diana coming into the front of the store right now," Officer Burns interjected, stepping a little farther away from the office and out into the store to get a better view. "It looks like Dwayne Skinner is with her."

"Well, hello," Diana called out to Melanie when she walked into the office. "I apologize for not calling you back. I didn't check my voice mail messages until a couple of minutes ago."

Dwayne walked in behind her, carrying a couple of large posters mounted on cardboard. "Good evening," he said to Melanie, followed by a polite nod toward Officer Burns.

He seemed more subdued than usual. Like Peter did. There was none of his usual banter, asking Melanie how her sales numbers were looking, offering free market advice and badgering her to go into business with him. But then, like Peter, he had been interviewed and must realize he was considered a possible suspect.

"Dwayne's promoting a big Winter Wonderland Crafts Show down in Spokane in a few weeks," Diana said to Melanie. "The Mercantile is joining forces with him. Let me know if you're interested in having me sell some of your jewelry there."

Melanie nodded. "That would be fantastic." She told Diana about her plans to move her larger pieces of furniture in a couple of days.

"You can set those over there," Diana said to Dwayne, gesturing toward her desk. As he set the posters down, a piece of paper slid off Diana's desk and fluttered to the floor. She leaned over to pick it up. "Actually you should have this," she said to Melanie, handing over the paper.

It was a notice from a package delivery company, telling her that some of the jewelry supplies Melanie had recently ordered were being returned to the shipper.

"I told the delivery man that you didn't do business here anymore and I didn't know exactly when you would be in the store again," Diana said. "I gave him your home address, but he said the package was sent with restricted delivery and couldn't be rerouted."

"No," Melanie said, her heart sinking with disappointment. She'd wanted to get started working on some jewelry as quickly as possible. She needed something productive to focus on rather than sitting around Anna's big house, worrying about when the next attack would happen. Not to mention worrying about what had triggered the light outside the kitchen door to come on last night. Melanie and Luke had looked at the security video several times, but there was no image captured of what had made that light turn on.

Melanie knew about the restricted delivery because some of the metals and gemstones in her order were fairly valuable and the supplier she'd ordered them from had insisted on scrupulous tracking of the items. She must have had the package delivered to The Mercantile instead of Anna's house out of habit.

She quickly found the contact information for the supplier on her phone and called them. The person she spoke with agreed to call the delivery company and ask them to hold the package at their office, which was located at the regional airport, several miles out of town.

When she disconnected, Officer Burns, who'd obviously overheard the conversation, frowned. "The airport is outside city limits. Sorry, but I can't drive with you out there. I'm on duty and I need to be able to respond to emergency calls in town."

"I can take you," Dwayne offered. "I left some things in my plane that I've been meaning to retrieve and take home."

Not a chance.

"Thank you for the offer, but I'll have to

decline," Melanie said politely. "I have to be cautious right now. I'm sure you understand."

"Of course," he said. He flashed her that easy, winning smile she'd seen so often on his billboards and other advertisements. "But if you think of anything I can do for you, let me know."

"Of course."

She started digging around in her purse for her phone.

"I appreciate you doing this for me," Melanie said from her seat in the truck beside Luke. She held her hands toward the vent in front of her, where warm air was blowing. A light, icy rain was falling outside.

"I'm happy to do it," Luke said. All things considered, that was true. He certainly didn't want anyone else driving her out to the airport.

Asking her to simply wait for the packages to be re-sent to Anna's house hadn't struck him as necessarily the safest option.

Maybe he was overthinking things, but having packages delivered to the house right now seemed risky. The explosion at the storage place told them the assailant knew how to make a bomb. Or at least how to get one. And now that Melanie had officially closed up shop at The Mercantile and was opening her online business, packages were one obvious way the attacker could get to her.

If Luke had his way, he'd take Melanie back to the ranch and hide her there until this case was solved and he knew for certain the danger was over. But he had to admit her concern about putting Alan and Kayla in danger was well reasoned. And demonstrated her selflessness.

The woman had heart. And for a guy who'd never been terribly social, he found her easy to be around. Even now, when it seemed like every nerve he had was on edge as he kept an eye out for possible threats, he felt like he could make it through any challenge he faced, as long as he had her by his side.

"It's just that I need to get some jewelry made and quickly distributed to retailers if I want to sell it during the Christmas shopping season," she said. "It will be here before you know it."

"Of course." Luke had already figured out she was a nervous chatterer. She'd mentioned this same exact concern twice since he'd received her call, taken off work early, and had a coworker drop him off at The Mercantile to meet her and get his truck.

Of course she was nervous. Her anxiety had been building since the initial attack. And with good reason.

Luke was nervous, too. He was nervous about this trip to the airport. Yet it was entirely possible that Melanie was safer here, riding with him in his truck, than she would be back at the house. Bowen was a small town and he had no doubt the assailant knew where Melanie lived. In fact he was fairly certain the motion-sensor light had been triggered last night by someone trying to figure out the extent of Anna's home security system. Melanie didn't want to leave town, but for the sake of her safety they needed to consider that option. The obvious question was, where could she go that they could be certain she'd be safe?

"Did you learn any new information about my case today?" Melanie asked. Her voice sounded shaky. He looked over and saw that she was trembling. The heater was turned up and he was fairly sure her chill wasn't from the cold. It was fear and exhaustion taking its toll.

He opened his mouth to answer when he heard a loud *bang*, and the truck suddenly pulled hard to the right. The front passenger-side tire had blown out. He fought the wheel to keep the lurching truck on the road when he heard a second bang. The shatter-proof glass mostly held together, but there was a chunk of the driver's-side window that was suddenly gone.

A shooter!

"Get down!" Keeping one hand on the wheel, he reached for Melanie's arm and pulled her sideways toward the seat, desperate to get her out of the shooter's line of fire.

Determined to figure out where the shots were coming from, he looked all around but didn't see another vehicle on the road.

An ambush. Someone must have been lying in wait for them in the dark forest alongside the two-lane road. He had to keep the truck moving. If they stopped they'd be sitting ducks.

He jammed his foot down on the gas pedal and forced the truck to continue forward, but it moved slowly, heaving from side to side as it crawled along. The front passenger tire was completely flat and they were riding on the rim. In the truck's back seat, the stacks of Melanie's jewelry in plastic storage boxes rattled and slid around.

Luke grabbed his phone and shoved it toward Melanie. "Call for help!"

Determined not to stop, he fought to keep the truck going until it took a sudden lurch and slid sideways on the thin layer of ice collecting on the road. He furiously turned the wheel but his efforts were useless. The truck slid past the edge of the asphalt and the wheels got bogged down in the mud. He threw it into reverse gear but that didn't get them unstuck. He shifted into low gear and tried to move forward, but that didn't work, either.

Beside him, he heard Melanie yelling, "Hello! Hello!" into his phone. "I can't get any reception," she finally said, shaking her head. "I'll try my own phone."

The attacker had picked the perfect spot for his attack. They were in the mountains, in a low depression between two ridgelines. Reception would be decent farther up the road, or even behind them, but not right here.

"Nothing on my phone, either," Melanie said, her voice sounding flat and defeated.

"Well, we can't wait here." Luke turned off the engine and the truck's headlights. He felt for the reassuring weight of his service weapon. Then he took off his jacket, handed it to Melanie and told her to put it on over the coat she was already wearing. He grabbed the heavy flashlight he kept beside the driver's seat. "Hold on to the phones," he told her. "Don't lose them."

"What are we going to do?" she asked, sitting up and shrugging into his jacket.

"We're getting out and we're going for a hike." He kept his voice calm. Made a point of sounding like he wasn't particularly worried. "We shouldn't have to go far to get phone reception." This would be a terrifying situation for anybody, so he braced himself for Melanie's response. He couldn't afford to spend too much time calming her down if she panicked.

In fact she simply looked at him and nodded. "Okay, let's go."

Luke reached past her to shove open the door on the passenger side, working on the theory that since the driver's-side window had been shot out, that was the side of the road the shooter was on. But there were no guarantees. The shooter could have moved to the other side of the road by now.

He gestured at Melanie to slide out, and then he scooted across the bench seat and climbed out behind her.

The icy rain was still falling, hitting the road with a pattering sound.

And then Luke heard the low rumbling sound of a vehicle moving up the road. It was coming from the direction of Bowen. The same direction they'd just traveled.

"Come on!" Luke grabbed Melanie's arm and pulled her toward the trees on the side of the road where they could hide out of view.

"Maybe it's someone who will help us!" she said excitedly.

"Maybe," he said. Or maybe it was the shooter. Or an accomplice of the shooter. They had no proof that the assailant was acting alone.

Headlights rounded a twist in the road, washing Luke's disabled truck in light, and then the vehicle stopped. It stayed on the road, with the engine idling.

After a few seconds it crept forward a little. And in the backwash of the illumination from the headlights, the front of the rig became visible.

"That truck looks familiar," Melanie whispered.

It looked familiar to Luke, too. He readied his gun, flicking off the safety, just in case. Then he pointed his flashlight toward the windshield of the truck and turned it on.

Beside him, he heard Melanie draw in a sharp breath. "Peter?"

It was indeed Peter Altman sitting behind the wheel, staring toward the source of the bright light shining in his face, his expression baffled. Was he the perpetrator of the ambush, surprised to get caught?

Multiple gunshots rang out from the dark forest, with the bullets shattering the windshield of Peter's truck. Luke immediately extinguished his flashlight, but not before seeing Peter collapse and fall over. His truck jolted forward until it hit a sturdy tree and then stopped with the engine whining.

The icy rain felt like small, sharp blades running down the surface of Melanie's skin. And yet somehow, at the same time, she felt numb. It was all too much. From the attempts on her life, to seeing young Peter Altman face a hail of bullets.

Two weeks ago, when she'd awoken in the woods outside the fairgrounds, Melanie's world had stopped making sense. She'd tried holding herself together, but right now she'd endured all she could take and she was falling to pieces.

But then she felt Luke standing close beside her, warm and strong. He wrapped a muscled arm around her shoulder. "Some-body will come by and call the police," he said. "Let's wait here for a few minutes. I don't want to break cover in case the shooter is lurking nearby, waiting to get a clear shot at you."

"But Peter?" Melanie said softly. "Do you think he could have survived that?"

Luke didn't answer. Just held her tighter. She supposed that meant his answer was *no*.

Why was Peter on this road? He didn't live out this way. Her mind tried to unravel the knotted question of what he was doing out here.

"Peter knew I wanted to pick up my jew-elry supplies tonight," she said. She should have kept her plans to drive out here secret. But she was new to being paranoid. "Do you think he told the shooter I was coming out here? And then maybe the shooter betrayed Peter and shot him so he couldn't ever iden-tify the shooter to the police?"

"It's possible," Luke said. "It could be that he was working with his criminal family. It could be that something completely different was going on. We still have a whole lot of questions and not much in the way of answers."

So, what did that mean Melanie's future would be like? Would she be scared and in hiding for the rest of her life?

She blew out a breath. *Dear Lord, help.*

She heard a metallic squeaking sound, and she was sure the bad guys had found them. Luke lifted his gun. And then she realized the passenger door of the truck was opening from the inside.

Could Peter possibly be alive? If he was, they had to help him no matter what he'd done.

"We need to check on him," Luke whispered in her ear, apparently thinking along the same lines she was.

"Let's go."

He took her hand and they hurried to the

truck, sliding on the slippery road. Luke pulled open the door. Warm air drifted out of the cab. Peter was half sitting and half lying on the passenger side of the bench seat. He looked at them, eyes wide. "W-what's happening?" he asked. In the light cast by the truck's instrument panel, Melanie could see that there were cuts on his face from the broken glass, and a dark bloodstain on his shoulder where he must have been struck by a bullet.

"You tell us," Luke said sternly as he and Melanie crouched beside the truck, using the vehicle's body and the open door for protection in case the shooter decided to open fire on them again. "What are you doing here?"

"Peter," Melanie said. "Why have you been trying to kill me?"

"I haven't been," he answered in a voice that was nearly a wail. "I wanted to protect you. I heard you talk about coming out here tonight and I thought I'd ride out behind you just to keep an eye on things. I was farther behind you than I wanted to be because I had to stop and put gas in my truck."

Luke stood up and leaned into the truck to check Peter's wound. "It's not bleeding too badly," he told Peter. "Try not to move any more than you have to."

"Okay."

"Your truck engine's still running," Luke said. He turned to Melanie. "Get in, and let's get out of here."

He turned to Peter. "Sit up and move back so Melanie can climb over you. I'll drive and I want her next to me. If you make the slightest move toward her, do anything that looks like a threat to her, I will shoot you."

"Yes, sir."

Luke hurried around the front of the truck and got into the driver's seat. He threw the truck in Reverse and backed away from the tree where the truck had come to rest. He got the vehicle back onto the road. And then two bright lights flashed on in the darkness.

The lights were on the road ahead of them.

Vehicle headlights. Like a predator in the darkness suddenly opening its eyes. The shooter had been waiting. Maybe he hadn't been able to see Melanie and Luke in the steadily falling sleet when they were on foot, but he saw them now that they were in Peter's truck.

"Try calling again for help," Luke said to Melanie as he whipped the truck around and got it facing the opposite direction, toward Bowen.

The predator vehicle was behind them now, in the middle of the road, barreling down on them with its high beams on.

Luke jammed his foot on the gas pedal, but Peter's truck only limped along. Clearly the engine had been damaged in that hail of gunfire earlier, but they hadn't realized it until now.

The vehicle behind them was getting closer, its bright lights shining through the cab's rear window.

Melanie reached for the two phones she'd

tucked into the deep pockets of Luke's coat. She shoved one at Peter. "Call 9-1-1!"

There was a hard slam to the back of the truck. The predator vehicle had rammed into them, and the impact knocked the phone out of Peter's hand. He bent over and pawed at the floorboard, trying to grab it. Melanie punched the emergency numbers on her own phone.

Meanwhile Luke fought to keep the damaged truck on the road as the assailant behind them bashed into them yet again. They were nearing a bridge over a narrow fork of the Bowen River. On the other side was a gas station with a small store. "The store should still be open," Luke said. "Maybe the possibility of having several witnesses will be enough to get this idiot behind us to back off."

Melanie thought she got a connection on her phone. The ringing on the other end of the call had stopped, so maybe someone had answered, but she wasn't sure. The damaged truck was clattering and squeaking—the noise was especially loud through holes in the windshield—and on her phone she could hear a lot of static.

If an operator had said something to her, she hadn't heard it. Melanie was afraid anyone listening would have trouble hearing her, so she yelled into the phone, giving their location on the highway, telling them what was happening, pleading for help. Pressing the phone closer to her ear, she listened for a response.

A sudden hard bash from the back sent the truck sliding across the icy road and over the embankment, right where the bridge across the river connected to the road. "Hold on!" Luke yelled as he wrestled with the steering wheel for control. But the momentum was too much and he couldn't keep the truck from leaving the road. It careened over grass and pine needles, rumbling down the embankment, spinning and sliding a short distance before finally coming to a stop, now facing the opposite direction, just short of hitting the water.

"Everybody okay?" he called out when the movement finally stopped.

Before anyone could answer, the vehicle that had been pursuing them turned off the pavement and onto the mud and grass, driving straight toward them, blinding them with its bright headlights. And then it stopped.

"What is he doing?" Melanie asked.

"He's going to ram into us again!" Luke shouted.

He shoved open his door and got out, then reached for Melanie and helped her out. "Come on!" he called out to Peter.

Peter barely moved. Melanie grimaced when she saw how much more blood there was now on his shirt. All of that jostling around must have made his bullet wound worse.

Luke started climbing back into the truck to help him.

Melanie suddenly felt herself being

yanked backward. Someone had grabbed her hair and was pulling her. The attacker clamped a hand over her mouth so she couldn't scream.

He dragged her for several yards, through the mud and the falling sleet. She could no longer see Luke, Peter's truck or even the predator vehicle with the bright headlights.

Melanie struggled and fought as best she could, but it did her no good. She couldn't get away. Terror and exertion had her gasping for air. Her heart was pounding so hard, it felt like it would burst out of her chest. A feeling of hopelessness began to worm its way into her thoughts.

Finally the dragging stopped. "You've laughed at me before. But I don't hear you laughing now," a familiar voice said into her ear. And then the hand was removed from her mouth. The grip that held her tight was loosened. And she could finally see Dwayne Skinner. He flashed her his signature rodeo-champ smile.

"Laughing?" Melanie said, trying to catch her breath. And trying to get over her shock and confusion. *Dwayne Skinner?* Why was he doing this? What was going on? "Laugh at you?" she said. "I've never done that. Why would I laugh at you?"

"Ah, now I hear respect in your voice," Dwayne said, still smiling.

Respect? What was he talking about?

Melanie shivered uncontrollably, both from the freezing-cold weather and from a spike of fear. She'd just seen the gun in his hand.

"I've always respected you," she said in a shaky voice. She'd had no reason not to.

"You thought I was washed-up," he said, the smile disappearing from his face. "You thought I had nothing left to offer because I wasn't a rodeo champ anymore. You thought I was an aging joke with my late-night TV commercials and my billboards."

Melanie couldn't figure out the point of his ramblings, and right now she didn't care.

She just needed to get away. But he had that gun. And it was pointed at her.

"You're like those other nobodies who thought they were better than me and laughed at me."

Other *nobodies*? So, Dwayne *had* attacked those women in Wyoming and Montana. He'd murdered one of them. It looked like Melanie was going to be next.

But what would make him think she'd laughed at him? She couldn't think of a single instance when she'd done that. "Is this about me turning down your offer to go into business together?" she asked, grasping at the only time she could think of when they'd had any kind of a conflict. "That wasn't disrespect for you. That was about me wanting to have my own business. Wanting to be independent." She forced herself to sound calm and reasonable. Maybe she could defuse the situation by talking.

"Liar," he sneered. "Right now you'll say anything to save yourself."

"Dwayne Skinner, let her go!" Luke called out from the darkness.

At the sound of Luke's voice, Melanie felt a surge of hope, even though she couldn't see him. He'd found her! Despite the darkness and the thick forest and the relentless falling sleet, he'd found her.

"We can hear your voice, Dwayne," Luke called out again. "We know it's you. Don't make things worse for yourself. Let Melanie go."

Dwayne snatched Melanie's hand and started pulling her farther into the woods. Seconds later a bright beam of light from a flashlight shone on their faces. "You're not going anywhere," Luke shouted.

Peter's voice called out from the opposite direction. "Let her go, Skinner!"

Dwayne had let the hand that was holding his gun fall to his side. He began to lift it.

"Drop your weapon!" Luke commanded.

Dwayne ignored him, turning the barrel to point it toward Melanie's head.

In the quiet of the woods, the shot that followed sounded like an explosion.

THIRTEEN

"And then Luke, I mean Lieutenant Baxter, shot him," Melanie said. She was in an office at the Sheriff's Department, giving her statement about what had happened tonight. Or maybe it had happened last night. It could be past midnight by now.

"For the record tell me exactly who it was that Lieutenant Baxter shot." Of course this conversation was being recorded. The woman questioning Melanie was a sergeant in the neighboring Korman County Sheriff's Department. It was protocol in Miles County for an outside agency to investigate any officer-involved shooting. So that meant she had to tell the story of what had happened all over again, to this new investigator.

Melanie looked down at the damp white tissues in her hands. While sitting here, answering the sergeant's questions, she'd torn them to shreds. She'd burst into tears several times during the night. The first time was when she'd been overcome with terror as Luke had fired his service weapon and the whole world seemed to explode. Then again, a little later in the evening, she'd cried tears of relief when the realization had sunk in that the terror of the last two weeks was over at last. Finally she'd felt tears rolling down her cheeks again after she'd been brought back to the station and separated from Luke. She'd missed him immediately and had been overwhelmed by a feeling of hollowness and heartache. That last pain was the worst and still had her teary-eyed. Because she was pretty sure that pain was never going to end.

Melanie glanced up and realized the sergeant was waiting for her response. "Lieutenant Baxter shot Dwayne Skinner," she said. "Dwayne had a gun pointed at my head. He was going to kill me."

"And at that point the other officers arrived?"

"Yes," Melanie said. Apparently the 9-1-1 call she wasn't sure about had in fact connected with an operator. Those moments after Dwayne had put the gun to her head had a dreamlike quality to them. There was the explosive sound of the gunshot. The deadweight of Dwayne collapsing onto her and knocking her to the cold, sleet-covered forest floor. Then the sensation of Luke helping her to her feet and wrapping his arms around her, the exhalations of his breath blowing warmly across the top of her head.

He'd said a bunch of things to her, but for the life of her, she couldn't remember what they were. Eventually he'd loosened his hold on her. At that point, through the falling sleet, she'd been able to see the watery red-and-blue flashing lights from the approaching cop cars.

An ambulance followed behind them. By now she knew that Peter had already undergone surgery for his bullet wound and that he was resting comfortably.

"Based on what you've told us about Dwayne Skinner admitting to the attacks on the other women, plus further information and evidence collected by law enforcement agencies in Wyoming and Montana, I'm confident we'll get a conviction against Mr. Skinner."

"So, Luke's shot didn't kill him?" Taking a life would not be easy on Luke, even if he was forced by circumstances to do so.

"No. Skinner is in the hospital, but he's expected to recover." The sergeant leaned back in her chair. "I think that's enough for now. We'll probably need to ask you a few more follow-up questions in the future, but that's normal for an investigation like this." She got to her feet. "Meanwhile is there someone here waiting for you? Otherwise I can have a deputy drive you home."

Melanie stood and tossed her damp tissues into a wastebasket. "I haven't called anyone yet." She'd sent Anna a brief text, telling her that she was with Luke and that she'd be late getting home. Her cousin might be offended when she discovered that Melanie hadn't called her immediately after Skinner was arrested, but she was overwhelmed at the time and could only do so much. If she called her now, Anna would certainly come to the station and pick her up. Likewise any of her church friends would come down to the station and help her no matter how late the hour.

But there was only one person she wanted to see right now.

"Is Lieutenant Baxter still here?" she asked, forcing herself to look the sergeant in the eyes, even as she felt a flush of embarrassment warm her cheeks. Maybe she should pretend to be more aloof than she actually felt. Maybe she was in danger of looking like a cop groupie with a crush on the man who had helped keep her safe.

But she didn't care if she looked like a fool. She'd told herself if she ever had another serious romantic relationship, she would insist on it being with a man who would honestly communicate with her.

Well, maybe she needed to be the one to take that first step. And it couldn't wait any longer. Because her case was now solved, and that meant Luke would be moving out of Anna's house. In fact there was no reason for him not to return to the ranch whenever he left here tonight. After that it was unlikely she and Luke would cross paths again.

"Lieutenant Baxter is also being interviewed right now," the sergeant said, escorting Melanie out of the office, through the squad room and toward the lobby. "I don't know how long it will take. Could be a while. Why don't I have someone take you home? I'll give Luke the message that you'd like to speak with him."

After all she and Luke had been through together, especially tonight, with Skinner nearly succeeding in killing her, she *needed* to see him. There would be no point in going home and trying to sleep without doing that. A few minutes with Luke was the only thing that could possibly calm her racing mind.

"I'll wait for him," she said.

Nervous energy kept her from sitting in one of the padded chairs in the lobby, so she stepped outside, anticipating a blast of cold air. Instead a much warmer breeze was blowing. The piles of sleet on the road had turned into puddles of water. That sometimes happened this time of year, before true winter set in. The weather could suddenly change. And you just had to roll with it.

Stars were visible in the night sky, just like they'd been when Luke had first come to her rescue in the woods by the fairgrounds. She was still thinking about that night when she heard the door open and close behind her.

"You waited for me." It was Luke.

"Of course." She took a deep breath and turned around. And then she just stood there, staring at him. Because despite her best intentions, she couldn't think of anything to say. She was caught up in what she *felt*, and it was a struggle to put words to that. Longing, maybe. Compassion. Gratitude. Delight.

Love. What she felt for Luke was love. The crystal-clear reality of that terrified her.

"I'm glad you're here," Luke said.

"I'm glad you're here, too."

The man looked like he'd been through the wringer. She'd already seen herself in a mirror and she knew she looked even worse. Still, in his eyes she saw the steadfast spirit she so admired. Standing here with him, she felt both calm and filled with nervous energy at the same time.

"I'm not going anywhere," he said, watching her closely. He held out both his hands.

Not quite sure what he intended, Melanie reached out and grasped them. They were big and warm and a little bit calloused.

"I'm glad you're all right," he said.

"Me, too."

"But I'm not all right," he added.

She stared at him, confused. Why was he talking in riddles? And why was she suddenly so tongue-tied? She'd been the one determined to have a steady flow of honest conversation in any future romantic relationship. And yet here she was, at a loss for words.

Luke took a deep breath. And the earnest expression on his face shifted into a shy, self-conscious smile. "What I mean is that I'm not going anywhere. I'm not leaving town unless you leave town."

He shook his head, looked up at the stars, then looked back at her. This time his expression was more serious. "I've been restless for my whole life, it seems. Looking for something to take my mind off feeling alone. Looking for situations that were life-or-death. Searching for experiences that would give me a surge of adrenaline that would empty my mind of everything except the mission at hand. Because that would give me peace." He sighed deeply. "I was searching for what was missing in my life through those experiences. And then I met you."

The quivering sensation in Melanie's stomach got ten times worse. Tears began to form in her eyes.

"There's a whole lot we don't ever get to understand in life," he continued. "But sometimes there are things we *know*. And I know you're the woman for me."

Melanie felt herself smile. Felt tears begin to roll down her face. A year ago, a week ago, ten minutes ago, she would not have been able to imagine how things could possibly work together for this moment to arrive. And yet here it was.

"I couldn't say anything until now because you were obviously involved in a case I was working on and there are professional standards I have to follow. But that situation has now changed." He looked down at their hands, which were still joined together, then back into Melanie's eyes. "I know this isn't a romantic time or place, but I can't let another minute go by without knowing that you will always be in my life. I love you, Melanie. Will you marry me?"

She burst into full-blown, gushing tears.

Luke looked alarmed.

She couldn't help it. For the moment she couldn't even speak. It was like an emotional logjam had burst open, and love and joy and hope for the future flooded her heart.

She nodded her head, but Luke still looked concerned. And then she realized she'd barely said a word since he'd come outside. He'd done all the talking. Given her what she'd wanted. Told her how he honestly felt.

"Yes!" she finally said. "I love you, too! Yes, I will marry you!"

The expression of concern on his face shifted to a smile. "I've been waiting way too long to do this." He leaned forward for a kiss.

The press of his lips was warm and comforting. He let go of Melanie's hands and then placed his hands on either side of her waist. Slowly he slid them toward the small of her back, pulling her tighter against his chest as he continued kissing her.

Melanie's heart raced while she melted into his embrace and felt his protective arms wrap around her. This was exactly where she was supposed to be.

EPILOGUE

Two months later

"I'm so happy I finally got to meet Billy Clyde," Anna said, smiling at Kayla and Alan while she gave their scruffy dog a couple of good scratches between his ears.

Luke's niece and nephew, along with three other children, were sitting on the floor in the front room of Anna's house, decorating wooden sticks and using them to make picture frames. Billy Clyde was lying on the floor, in the middle of them, and at the sound of his name he wagged his tail.

"Oh, sure, you're a good boy at somebody else's house," Jake said to the dog, trying to sound stern but unable to shake the smile from his face. He directed his gaze at Anna. "You should see how he behaves at home."

Melanie grinned. Her heart felt light and festive.

Seated beside her on the couch, Luke gave her hand a squeeze. He liked to hold hands. He liked to plan for their future together. And he liked to talk about how many children they might have and what kind of dad he wanted to be. A very involved one, as it turned out. He'd made that quite clear. As Melanie had recently learned, most of the people who knew Luke were certain he'd never get married. He seemed to enjoy surprising them.

Tonight's special occasion was Melanie and Luke's engagement party. The wedding would be in July, at the ranch, when the weather was better. But they didn't want to wait to celebrate, and Anna had been delighted when they'd asked if they could have a few close friends over to her house for a nice, relaxed, buffet-style dinner. Anna had come up with the craft idea to keep the kids busy. She'd said she needed the practice. Tyler was on track to return home soon and they were planning on starting a family. "Maybe our children can play together like you and I did when we were kids," she'd said to Melanie, and Melanie had burst into tears. She'd been doing a fair amount of happy crying lately.

"Anna, where do you keep your coffee filters?" Tanya called out from the kitchen.

"I should go help her," Melanie said, getting to her feet. She was very aware of how much people had done for her when she was terrified and desperate and not especially easy to get along with.

She'd thought about that a lot since Dwayne Skinner was formally charged with the attempts on her life. There would be more charges coming for the attacks in Wyoming and Montana, and the trial was a long way off.

As it turned out Dwayne had made a point

of driving to the locations where he'd attacked those other women rather than flying his plane, so that he wouldn't leave an evidence trail. All of the women he'd hurt had turned down a business-related offer or request by him and he'd interpreted that as an insult that could not go unanswered. But he would not get away with his crimes, despite his claims that he'd been goaded into them by women who'd treated him disrespectfully and laughed at him.

His first attempt on Melanie's life at the fairgrounds had been triggered by her refusal to go into business with him. He'd waited to attack her until he was certain he could get away with it. He thought he'd shot and killed her in the woods outside the fairgrounds. It wasn't until later that evening that he'd learned his shot had broken a tree branch and that the branch had hit her, knocking her unconscious. She had not been felled by the actual shot he'd fired. After that, he'd made further attempts to finish the job.

Then he'd heard about her amnesia and figured he'd kill her before she regained her memory and was able to identify him as the assailant. He'd never realized that she'd recovered her memory but still couldn't identify him as her attacker because she'd never gotten a good enough look at him.

Luke followed Melanie into the kitchen, where she chatted with Tanya and a friend from church while she started a pot of coffee brewing. "Look," he said, pointing out the kitchen window. "It's starting to snow."

It was a little early in the season for snow, but there it was.

Suddenly the house felt a little too crowded for Melanie. Or maybe she just wanted a few minutes alone with her future husband. They didn't spend nearly as much time together as she'd like. He had moved back to the ranch and he still worked long hours. She spent a lot of time here at the house, getting her online business going. She'd gone back to renting space at The Mercantile and put Peter in charge of managing that for her. He was also in charge of selling her merchandise at rodeos and craft fairs around the region. Melanie was finished with traveling long distances to those events. She wanted to stay close to home.

Peter had proven himself more than trustworthy and she no longer doubted him. Not even after his brothers were arrested for dealing in stolen goods. They'd been afraid that Luke was onto that criminal endeavor, and that was why they'd been so determined to avoid his questioning. But eventually he'd caught them, anyway.

"Let's go outside for a minute," she said to Luke.

He walked with her out the side door and toward the front porch, holding her hand. Once they were on the porch, she leaned against the railing and looked up and down the street. A light layer of snow covered everything now, making it all look pristine and brand-new.

"You've been quiet tonight," she said.

"You're not going to make me talk about my feelings, are you?" he asked dryly. "Okay, I'm very happy. I'm enjoying this evening, and I'm very much looking forward to marrying you." He pulled her toward him for a slow, lingering kiss. Then he wrapped his arms around her and rested his chin atop her head. They stayed that way for a couple of minutes, until regretfully Melanie pulled away.

"We should get back to our guests."

"Whatever you want."

That was the amazing thing. She'd gotten exactly what she wanted, even when she hadn't known what that was. She'd gotten Luke and this chance for a new life together. She'd gotten reassurance that the fears she'd wrestled with—that she'd completely messed up her life and her chance at her own family—were unfounded.

She glanced at the warm lights spilling out of the windows at the front of Anna's house, listened to the laughter and excited voices of her friends and family inside, and then looked at the loving, compassionate, brave and faith-filled man who would soon be her husband. Her life path may have been meandering, and it may have taken her through some turns she would never have willingly chosen, but it had truly brought her home.

* * * * *

Dear Reader,

A new start in life can be a tricky thing.

Maybe it's something you wanted and you're excited, but also nervous.

Or maybe it's something you never saw coming and you certainly didn't ask for it.

Either way they're an inevitable part of life.

Both Melanie and Luke were faced with changes in their lives, which meant they had to navigate unforeseen twists and turns in their paths. And then, to add to their stress, someone tried to kill Melanie! It's amazing to me how often trouble shows up in bunches. When that happens to me, I try to handle the situation the way Melanie and Luke did. I try to take care of the practical challenges as best I can. And for the rest, I press on in faith.

I enjoy connecting with my readers. You can find me at my website, JennaNight.com, on my Jenna Night Facebook page or you can follow me on Twitter, @Night_Jenna. My email address is Jenna@JennaNight. com. I'd love to hear from you. And I hope the new starts in your life lead you to greater faith, peace and love.

Jenna Night